"I'm trying to save you from yourself."

"I don't need saving," Morgan insisted.

"Might I remind you of the stunts you pulled at the wedding?" Jared replied. "Your big revelation. Getting drunk. Attempting to spend the night with a complete stranger."

"You're not a stranger anymore. I know your full name now. Jared Robinson."

Jared couldn't resist smiling. "Yes, you do."

"So tell me, Mr. Robinson. Why did you leave without...?"

"Without making love to you?"

"Why? Any other man might have taken advantage."

"I'm not every other man."

"No, you're not."

"I'm glad. And I'm going to continue being a man of mystery by offering you a deal you can't refuse."

"And what's that?"

"I need a girlfriend. A very public one and I've decided you'd make a great one. So how about it?"

* * *

Secrets of a Fake Fiancée by Yahrah St. John is part of The Stewart Heirs series.

Dear Reader,

Secrets of a Fake Fiancée is the final book in The Stewart Heirs series. Originally, *Red Carpet Redemption* would have been the final book. However, the story felt incomplete. Henry Stewart was such an interesting father figure, it seemed natural he could have another child out there. Thus, the character of Morgan Stewart was born.

Feisty, independent Morgan is the outsider who desperately wants to be accepted by the Stewarts but doesn't go about it the right way. She meets her match in reluctant knight-in-shining-armor Jared Robinson, who bails her out of trouble. But she also finds the Robinsons, the family she always wanted, and love isn't far behind.

Can't wait for my next book? Never fear. *Insatiable Hunger*, book three in the Dynasties: Seven Sins series with several Harlequin Desire authors, debuts July 2020. Visit my website to stay current on YSJ news, www.yahrahstjohn.com, or write me, yahrah@yahrahstjohn.com.

Happy reading,

Yahrah St. John

YAHRAH ST. JOHN

SECRETS OF A FAKE FIANCÉE

HARLEQUIN
DESIRE

HARLEQUIN®
DESIRE™

Recycling programs for this product may not exist in your area.

ISBN-13: 978-1-335-20912-2

Secrets of a Fake Fiancée

Harlequin Enterprises ULC
22 Adelaide St. West, 40th Floor
Toronto, Ontario M5H 4E3, Canada
www.Harlequin.com

Printed in U.S.A.

Yahrah St. John is the author of thirty-two books and one deliciously sinful anthology. When she's not at home crafting one of her spicy romances with compelling heroes and feisty heroines with a dash of family drama, she is gourmet cooking or traveling the globe seeking out her next adventure. St. John is a member of Romance Writers of America. Visit www.yahrahstjohn.com for more information.

Books by Yahrah St. John

Harlequin Desire

The Stewart Heirs

At the CEO's Pleasure
His Marriage Demand
Red Carpet Redemption
Secrets of a Fake Fiancée

Harlequin Kimani Romance

Cappuccino Kisses
Taming Her Tycoon
Miami After Hours
Taming Her Billionaire
His San Diego Sweetheart

Visit her Author Profile page at
Harlequin.com for more titles.

You can also find Yahrah St. John on Facebook,
along with other Harlequin Desire authors,
at www.Facebook.com/harlequindesireauthors!

To my friend Kiara Ashanti for always encouraging me to *write, write, write*.

One

Morgan Young couldn't imagine a more perfect place for a wedding than this La Jolla beach on a spring evening. She was touched by the heartfelt vows her boss, Dane Stewart, had just shared with his new wife, Iris. The couple had pledged their undying devotion with their son, Jayden, standing by his father's side. The wedding was an especially happy occasion, considering Jayden was battling a rare form of acute lymphocytic leukemia, and finding the father he'd never met had provided him with the life-saving treatment he needed. Jayden had needed a bone marrow transplant and Dane's stem cells had been just what the doctor ordered. Morgan had played an instrumental part in bringing the boys' parents together.

Dane, however, had no idea of Morgan's true identity. She was his baby sister.

Over the last year working as his assistant, she'd kept it hidden. Morgan hadn't intended to remain mum this long. On her deathbed, her mother, Crystal Young, had finally told Morgan her father was Henry Stewart. Crystal had had an affair with him decades ago. Morgan wanted to get to know him, but then she'd done her homework and learned of the man's previous infidelities and his estrangement from her half brother Ayden. Morgan wondered if Henry ever considered the consequences of his actions.

She was going to find out tonight.

"Can I get a whiskey?" Morgan asked the bartender from where she'd been perched watching Dane and Iris cut the cake and share their first dance.

"That's an awfully strong drink," a deep masculine voice said from Morgan's side.

She cocked her head and her breath was stolen from her chest. The voice belonged to the most handsome man she'd ever seen. He had skin the color of shortbread, stunning smooth bone structure, midnight eyes framed by bushy brows and a wide sensual mouth. His hair was short and his tuxedo fit his tall frame perfectly. He towered over her. Morgan was five-seven, so she figured he was over six feet.

"I can handle my liquor."

He regarded her. "Is that right?" When she didn't respond, he looked at the uniformed bartender. "I'll have what the lady is having."

"Coming right up."

"So, what brings you here?" the stranger asked, turning to Morgan. "Are you a friend of the bride or the groom?"

"Both." Morgan sipped her whiskey.

"Really? I'm surprised Dane would have let a beautiful woman like you get away."

Morgan chuckled. "Dane and I are more like brother and sister." The stranger had no idea how true that statement was. "And he couldn't have picked a better wife. Iris is an amazing mother. The way she's dealt with Jayden's condition is nothing short of heroic. Jayden's very fortunate to have a mother like her in his corner."

The bartender returned with another glass and slid it toward the stranger. He accepted and drank a generous swallow. "Sounds like you speak from personal experience."

Morgan glanced at Henry Stewart, who was dancing with Fallon Stewart, Dane's sister. An ache formed in Morgan's chest. "I do." She downed the rest of her whiskey and placed it on the bar. "If you'll excuse me, I have some urgent business to attend to."

It was time she finally told Henry she was his daughter. Now was her chance.

Jared Robinson stared after the stunning beauty as he sipped his whiskey. *Who was she?* She claimed to know Dane and Iris, but he had never seen her before. Of course, the last time he'd seen Dane had been on a pit stop Dane made to Austin last year. He'd indicated he'd met someone, but hadn't gone into much detail. Jared didn't have to wait long to find out; as an A-list movie star and America's Sexiest Man Alive, Dane's every movement was tracked by the media. The press caught wind that Dane had fathered a child via sperm donation. Who could have predicted Jared's former running buddy would fall hard and fast for the mother of his child? But fall Dane had.

Jared had no intention of going down the wedded-bliss path. He was merely here on sufferance, paying his respects to his friend. He and Dane had once been the screwups of their respective families. When they were younger, they'd been rabble-rousers, constantly getting into trouble. His father, Clay, had thought putting Jared in a boarding school would tame him, but that only gave Jared more access to females.

Jared had a way with the ladies and was unapologetic about it. He liked them in all colors, shapes and sizes. But today, there wasn't anyone at the wedding who could hold a candle to the woman he'd shared a drink with.

Straight jet-black hair hung gloriously down the woman's back. She had caramel brown skin, big expressive hazel eyes and a beautiful full mouth tinted with peach gloss that Jared wouldn't mind placing his lips on. She wore a blush gown with crisscross spaghetti straps that showed off her slender back. She was easily about five foot six or seven with a lithe body. Jared wanted to get to know her better, but she'd rushed off. He would remedy the situation before the night was over. After suffering through Dane's wedding, Jared was entitled to a little fun and she was it.

Morgan was determined. Tonight, she would reveal her true identity to Henry Stewart. She had no idea how he would take her revelation, but it was time to find out.

She was thwarted by the wedding planner, who was now ushering the guests toward the front driveway to send off the happy couple in a classic Rolls-Royce decked with streamers. Morgan was swept away in the melee. She now stood near the car and was handed a sparkler. From her vantage point, Morgan saw Dane and Iris kiss Jayden and hug their families.

Morgan's eyes welled with tears. *She* should be standing over there with them. She shouldn't have waited so long to tell the Stewarts the truth. Maybe then she wouldn't feel like an outsider with her own family only a few feet away. She was about to push people aside, when Dane stepped away and came toward her. To Morgan's surprise, he wrapped her in his arms.

"You're part of the reason this was all possible," Dane whispered in her ear. "You helped get us back together. Thank you."

Morgan couldn't stop a tear from escaping. "You're welcome."

Seconds later, Dane was gone, helping Iris into the Rolls-Royce. Morgan watched her half brother drive away to his happily-ever-after. She sighed and then glanced up to see the rest of the Stewarts watching the car wistfully.

Now was her time. She had to seize it.

Smoothing her hands down her dress, she made her way toward them. Morgan's legs felt wobbly as if she were a newborn foal. Dane's sister Fallon and her husband, Gage, were chasing after their son, Dylan, who was always on the move. Morgan didn't see where Ayden and Maya had gone, but Henry and his wife, Nora, were still there in all their finery. Henry wore a tuxedo and Nora was in a one-shoulder black gown. Neither of them acknowledged her presence until Morgan cleared her throat.

"May I help you?" Nora asked, raising a brow.

Morgan ignored the look of disdain Nora gave her. Whitney, Dane's publicist, had hooked Morgan up with a designer who loaned her the dress she was wearing, so she wasn't sure why Nora was finding fault. "I was hoping to have a word with Mr. Stewart."

"Tonight is a time for family," Nora responded. "If you want to talk business, it will have to be another time."

"It's okay, Nora." Henry smiled down at his wife. "I can be magnanimous. I mean, Dane got married tonight. That is worth celebrating."

Nora sighed. "All right, but don't be long." She picked up the sides of her gown and walked toward the reception area.

"Thank you," Morgan said as she and Henry stepped away from the crowd and headed toward the beach. When they stopped, Morgan allowed herself time to really look at her father.

She'd seen only pictures, and although she'd studied them religiously trying to see parts of herself in the man, it was different seeing him in person. Henry had more salt than pepper in his closely cropped hair and his eyes were just like hers, hazel gray. Morgan figured her father was slightly under six feet, but no less impressive in her mind.

"All right, young lady, the floor is yours," Henry stated. "What can I do for you?"

Morgan swallowed. Her mouth felt dry and full of cotton. "Yes... I."

"Well? Spit it out. I don't have all day."

Although she'd waited her whole life for this moment, there was no easy way to say what she had to say. She just had to spit it out. "I'm your daughter."

Henry's eyes grew wide with alarm. "Excuse me?"

"You heard me," Morgan replied. "I'm your daughter."

"Like hell you are!" he bellowed. "I don't know what kind of game you're playing, young lady, but you're off the mark. My daughter *Fallon*—" he pointed across the lawn "—is standing over there."

"You have another," Morgan stated. "With Crystal Young. You met her in Las Vegas when she was performing as a showgirl at the Tropicana. You spent one night together and I'm the result."

"No, no!" Henry shook his head furiously. "You're wrong!" he yelled and then glanced around to see people were starting to watch their interaction, so he lowered his voice. "You don't know what you're talking about. I have never been unfaithful to my wife."

Morgan's ire rose. "C'mon, Henry. Nora wouldn't be the first wife you cheated on."

"So, what, you've done your research?" Henry huffed, "That means nothing. My first marriage with Lillian is public record."

Morgan noticed the crowd watching them had grown and Nora and Fallon were charging toward them. "So you're going to deny you spent the night with my mother at the Tropicana?

Henry glanced up at Nora, who was only a few feet away. "Yes. I don't know who you're talking about. You're mistaken."

"I'm not mistaken!" Morgan yelled. "You're my father."

A hush came over the crowd and suddenly even the

reception music paused. All eyes were on the two of them. Nora had a look of utter shock on her face while Fallon's was more of disbelief.

Henry headed toward his wife. "Nora!" But she was running through the grass. He turned to his daughter. "Fallon?"

Fallon held up her hand and shook her head. "I don't want to hear it, Daddy. Not now. I'm going after Mom." Seconds later, Morgan was left alone with her father.

Henry spun around to face Morgan. "You!" He pointed at her. "You did this! On what should have been one of the happiest days for our family, you come here and cause discord. I don't know who you are and I will never claim you as my daughter. You should leave because your presence is no longer wanted." Without another word, he raced after Nora.

Morgan stared at Henry's back as he literally ran away from her. When she could no longer see him, she looked up and saw everyone at the reception was watching her.

Everyone.

Waiting for her to do what? Make more of an embarrassment out of herself than she already had? Well, they were in for a rude awakening. The party was over. Lowering her head, Morgan shuffled away as fast as she could and went straight for the bar. As she walked by, the crowd parted like the Red Sea. As if she carried some sort of plague. And maybe she did. She was glad she'd at least waited for Dane and Iris's departure before confronting Henry.

Had she been hoping to be accepted with open arms? Of course not. But she hadn't expected complete and utter rejection, either.

When she made it to the bar, she eyed the bartender and mouthed the word *whiskey* to him. He understood and immediately came over with the bottle. When he began pouring the requisite two thumbs she motioned for him to continue. Only when the tumbler was full did she tell him to stop.

Morgan took a swift mouthful. The liquid burned going down and it felt good. She doubted it would wash away the stain of being humiliated, but it was a start.

"You didn't get the reaction you bargained for?"

Morgan glanced up at the stranger from earlier. Their exchange seemed like a lifetime ago even though it had been little more than a half hour since they'd shared a drink. She eyed him warily, noting he'd dispensed with his tie and undone several buttons on his shirt. "I'm in no mood for any commentary from the peanut gallery."

"Perhaps you should have had some earlier," he responded, his mouth quirking. "I could have told you you're timing for *that revelation* was lousy."

Morgan took another generous sip of her drink. "There was never going to be a right time. And I'd waited long enough."

"Apparently not long enough."

"Do you have to berate me? I've dealt with enough recriminations tonight."

He smiled. "Of course not. I'm sorry. How about we start over? My name is Jared."

"Jared." She turned to face him. It was hard to be angry at someone as good-looking as him. Morgan leaned over to clink her glass with his and saw it was empty. She motioned to the bartender. "Get Jared another drink. We're getting to know each other."

Jared was just the sort of distraction she needed to help her forget this terrible night.

Two

"My name is Morgan." The beauty gave Jared only her first name. He was surprised Morgan wanted to stay, considering how her father's rejection must have hurt and Henry had asked her to leave. She was licking her wounds and looking for a distraction and that was fine with Jared. He could use some unadulterated fun without any pesky emotional attachments. He didn't do serious.

His longest relationship had lasted three months. His girlfriends were short-term with a shelf life of a month. After the thrill in the bedroom was gone, it was on to the next beautiful woman. And Morgan wasn't just beautiful. There was a fragility to her, which spoke to his masculine side. He was no hero, but he wouldn't mind being *hers* for the night.

Another whiskey appeared and Jared accepted without hesitation. "It's a pleasure to meet you, Morgan." He tipped his tumbler to hers.

Their eyes met and held for endless seconds over the rim and Jared could swear he felt his stomach turn upside down. He was the first to look away and put down his glass. "How about a dance?"

"So everyone can watch me?" Morgan inquired, taking a large gulp of whiskey. "No, thank you."

"I'm sorry to tell you, but everyone was watching you the moment you announced to the world you were Henry Stewart's daughter."

A hint of a smile touched Morgan's lips. "I can't argue with that." She swallowed the remainder of the whiskey and took his hand.

"You need to go easy on the whiskey," Jared replied. "Otherwise, you'll have a helluva hangover tomorrow."

"I know what I'm doing."

Jared wasn't sure, but for some reason he felt compelled to stick around and find out.

Jared's hand threaded through Morgan's and a riot of sensations shot right through her belly like a fire to dry tinder. Morgan glanced up to see if Jared felt it too and he had. His eyes were dark and cloudy. Nervously, Morgan followed him onto the temporary wooden dance floor on the grass.

Jared pulled her into the center, ignoring all the openmouthed stares around them, placed his hands on her hips and began to move. Morgan wound her arms around his neck and joined in his sinuous rhythm. Jared was an excellent dancer.

"You're pretty good at this."

Jared flashed her a grin. "You're not bad yourself."

"I learned how to dance as a child."

He smiled as he thought of a young Morgan in ballet slippers. "Did you have a dance mom making you take ballet and tap? Or was it hip-hop?"

Morgan laughed. Her childhood was a far cry from what you saw on television. She didn't have Clair Huxtable from *The Cosby Show* as her mother. "Nothing as grandiose as that. I hung around backstage while my mom danced at the Tropicana in Vegas."

"Intriguing. I'm sure there's a story there." He used his thumb to push up her jaw and their eyes met. Attraction and lust were in those onyx depths.

"It's not one I plan on telling anytime soon."

"A woman with secrets," Jared surmised. "I like." He pressed forward until their bodies were flush.

Incendiary sexual heat slid up Morgan's spine. She wasn't used to this. Usually when things between her and a man heated up, she cooled off. But not tonight. Jared wasn't like other men she met. She dropped her nose to his chest and opened V of his tuxedo shirt. She inhaled his spicy scent. It was very intoxicating.

When he splayed his hand across her nearly bare back, Morgan stumbled, but Jared was right there, swaying them back and forth, pretending they were dancing. Morgan knew what this was—*it was seduction*. When his hands went lower and settled on her bottom, Morgan was shocked, but she didn't complain.

"You want to come to my room?" Morgan didn't know what possessed her to make such an outrageous proposition, but once it was out there, she couldn't take it back. With Jared, she didn't feel fearful like she did with other men. Maybe it would be okay to allow herself the one night. Maybe he could banish all the bad memories and she could finally be who she was meant to be.

Jared glanced down at her. "I don't know, Morgan. You've had a lot to drink and something tells me you don't normally operate this way."

Morgan glanced up at him in confusion. He could *tell* she was new at this? Was that why he wasn't rushing to take her up to her hotel room and have his wicked way with her? She'd already fumbled on revealing her true identity. Apparently, she couldn't even pick up a man, either.

She pushed away from him and Jared frowned. "Morgan, what's wrong?"

"I'm sorry to have bothered you. I was mistaken about your interest." She walked off the dance floor. She was grateful the crowd had begun to fade so no one witnessed her second rejection of the night. Morgan made her way back to the bar.

"Morgan, wait!" With his long strides, Jared caught up to her in no time. "It's not like that," he said when he finally met her back at the bar where she ordered another whiskey.

"Keep them coming until I tell you to stop," Morgan told the bartender, and slammed the entire glass down.

"Listen, Morgan. You've had a rough time tonight and I don't want to add to it by being a decision you regret in the morning."

"Then leave," Morgan replied. "I don't need a hero. I've been taking care of myself for a long time and to-night will be no different. So get lost, Jared."

Jared stared at her for several mind-churning seconds, turned on his heel and walked off. Good riddance, Morgan thought. He was probably too perfect to be her *first* anyway.

* * *

Jared wanted to ring Morgan's adorable neck. Drinking away her troubles wasn't going to solve anything, but was she willing to listen to the voice of reason? No.

And why was he being the voice of reason? *Because…* he'd never taken advantage of a woman in his life and he wasn't about to start now. Morgan was emotionally on the edge and well on her way to tying one on. Jared had been that way in his youth, but not anymore. And when he was *with* a woman, he wanted her to remember him when he was gone because he was nothing if not a giving lover.

He left her at the bar as she requested, but he didn't go far. Instead, he engaged in conversation with an acquaintance near the dance floor.

"So I hear you're working at Robinson Holdings," the older man said. Milton Brooks sat on the board of his family's company and often was in everyone's business.

"Yeah, in the marketing and public relations department."

"Your brother, Chris, has been making some big moves buying that La Shore development."

"Yes, well, Chris has an eye for such things," Jared said, keeping an eye on Morgan. He saw Pete Harris, an unscrupulous fellow from his and Dane's past, talking to Morgan, and Jared didn't like it one bit.

"He has a sharp eye, that brother of yours," the man said. "He's destined for big things."

His comment caught Jared's attention and rankled him. His older brother, Chris, was the favorite son, and it grated on Jared's nerves to hear the man's unabashed praise. Chris had been running Robinson Holdings since their father, Clay, unexpectedly stepped down due to a health crisis a year ago. Chris had doubled revenue and business was booming.

"Chris does seem to have the Midas touch," Jared replied. He turned in time to catch Pete putting his hand on Morgan's shoulder and her pushing him away. Pete wasn't taking no for answer and was getting handsy. "If you'll excuse me, I have some unfinished business to attend to," Jared said, taking his leave of the older man.

He quickly strode over to where Pete now had his hands wrapped around Morgan's waist. He caught the man by the collar and shoved him away.

"Hey…" Pete began, but stopped when he saw who it was. "Oh, hi, Jared." He held out his hand, but Jared glared at him, so he pulled it back. "Me and the little lady here were having a disagreement."

Jared turned to Morgan. Her face was flushed, and looking in her eyes he could see she was genuinely frightened. "Back off or I'll make you regret it."

Pete held up his hands. "I'm sorry." He quickly rushed off.

"Are you okay?" Jared asked, peering down at Morgan.

Morgan sucked in a deep breath. "Yeah, I'm okay now." She gave him a halfhearted smile, but he noticed her hand was shaking as she put her glass down on the bar. "Thanks for the assist."

"That's what heroes do." He offered her a wide grin.

"Well, thanks." She mussed with her hair for a few minutes, running her fingers through it, something Jared would sorely like to do. Then she turned back around and motioned to the bartender for another drink.

Jared stepped forward and put his hand over her empty glass. "You're done."

Her eyes flashed fire at him. "Just because you helped me out of a spot doesn't mean you get to tell me what to do."

"It does when you aren't capable of making good decisions. C'mon." He clasped her by the arm and started moving across the lawn toward the hotel entrance near the beach. "I'm going to walk you to your room and leave."

"Really?" Morgan asked mockingly as if she knew how much he wanted her and didn't believe for a second he'd walk away. "I doubt that." She stalked in front of him giving Jared a view of her delectable backside in her dress.

Damn her. She was not making it easy for him to walk away and do the right thing.

When they reached the bank of elevators, Morgan pressed the up button and they waited. The atmosphere was charged. When the elevator came, they both entered. It was empty and the air between them crackled with sexual tension. Morgan pressed the button for her floor and Jared went and stood on the other side of the car.

If he came any closer, he knew he would lose the control he was battling for. Need pulsed through every cell of his body. But he reminded himself Morgan wasn't like the other women he dated who knew the score. She was acting as if she did, but there was a certain naivete about her that told him he couldn't act on his desire.

The elevator bell chimed. They disembarked and

walked the short distance to her room. Morgan fished
a key from her clutch and opened the door.

"This is where I take my…" Jared never got to finish
because Morgan pulled him inside and shut the door.

Morgan didn't know what made her pull Jared into
her room. She just knew she had to. She craved his
touch and was desperate to know what he would taste
like. And if anyone could make her forget tonight, it
was Jared. When the door slammed, she suddenly
found herself pushing him back against it and angling
her head for a kiss. Her mouth covered his and she was
surprised to find his lips were deceptively gentle, lur-
ing hers into a sensual whirlpool.

"You really shouldn't have done that," Jared rasped,
lifting his head. Then he was drawing her closer until
their lower bodies touched, pelvis to pelvis. His hands
slid through the strands of her hair, then he lowered his
head and took. His lips ravished hers with gentle pressure before his tongue glided into her mouth and discovered every secret she'd kept hidden with other men.

Something unraveled inside Morgan, something
she'd long suppressed.

Lust.

She gave into the cascading shivers of desire by
linking her arms around his neck and leaning into him.
She loved the taste and feel of him. Jared's hands were
already sliding down her hips and holding her tightly
against his erection. Her breasts were pushed firmly
against his chest and she could feel the ridge of his
muscles underneath his tuxedo.

Jared groaned and his mouth engulfed Morgan's,
further spinning her senses out of control and making

her core contract with a need she'd never felt before. Whenever she got too close to a man, she clammed up, but not with Jared. First there was the dance and now this kiss. He had her under some sort of spell, so much so she was kissing him back with greedy fervor. Their tongues darted back and forth, dancing with each other in a brilliant tango Morgan never wanted to end. Jared had her entire body on fire. She wanted more, but like a cruel joke, her stomach churned.

She pushed away from Jared as quickly as she could and rushed toward the bathroom. Morgan made it in enough time to relieve her stomach of its contents. It was a horrible feeling knowing the sexy man of her dreams was on the other side of the door and she was retching because of the whiskey she'd imbibed earlier. He'd been right. She should have stopped while she was ahead and now she was going to pay the price.

Those were the last thoughts she remembered as she laid her head on the cold tile floor and passed out.

"Morgan?" Jared knocked on the bathroom door. She'd been in there a long time and there was no amount of exhaust fan noise to cover the sounds of her being sick. He'd tried to stop her from drinking too much her earlier, but she'd stubbornly refused to listen.

Jared ran his hands over his head. Fate had set the course of the night. When he'd walked Morgan to her room, he had every intention of leaving her at her door untouched. But when she'd pulled him in and kissed him, he'd lost all self-control. He wanted her with a burning ache that pulsed in his loins, even now. Jesus, he had to get the hell out of there, but first he had to make sure she was okay.

Easing the door open, he found Morgan on the floor. "Morgan!" He rushed over and checked for a pulse.

She was okay. Just seriously inebriated. Lifting her in his arms, Jared carried her into the bedroom and laid her on the bed. She looked so youthful and innocent in that blush dress, with her jet-black hair spread out over the pillow. Since she'd just gotten sick, Jared suspected Morgan would prefer to be out of the dress as to not soil it further.

Decision made. Jared reached behind her, unzipped the dress and pulled it over her head. Morgan barely moved a muscle. She was out like a light. But Jared had to suck in a deep breath. *She wasn't wearing a bra.* Her breasts were small and round, but enough for a handful. She had a flat stomach and shapely legs. A tiny scrap of material covered her femininity but did little to staunch his hunger. Quickly, he reached for the comforter and slid it over her naked yet beautiful body.

She was going to be hurting tomorrow. So he called room service. When a waiter delivered the bottled water and aspirin, Jared placed them on the nightstand, ensuring they'd be waiting for her tomorrow. Then he left the room. Once in the corridor, Jared leaned against the door and closed his eyes. He was thankful it had been him and not Pete. When she awoke the next morning, she'd know her hero, although tempted, had done the right thing.

Three

"Ugh!" Morgan clutched her pounding head as she rolled over in bed the next morning. "What time is it?" She glanced at the clock on the nightstand and saw it was nearly noon. She had slept the entire morning away. Memories from last night came flooding back. Henry's rejection at the reception. Her throwing back whiskey after whiskey. And then there was Jared.

Oh yes, she couldn't forget Jared.

The mysterious stranger who somehow made last night bearable. Morgan remembered their flirting, that first dance when they'd damn near dirty danced and then the amazing kiss up against her door. She glanced at the scene of the crime. When she closed her eyes, she could feel the pressure of his mouth, the glide of his lips against hers and then—the unthinkable.

She got sick. In the throes of her one and only make-out session with a hot guy, she'd ruined it by rushing off to the bathroom. But what happened afterward? She glanced at the space beside her; that side of the bed was untouched. Jared hadn't deigned to stay the night. Why would he? Sex was probably the last thing on his mind after witnessing her self-destruction. And she'd done it in epic proportion.

Glancing at the nightstand, she saw the bottled water and aspirin. She glanced upward and silently thanked Jared for his kindness. Swallowing two tablets, Morgan washed them down with water. He could have taken advantage in her weakened state, but he hadn't.

He'd been her hero.

Slowly, she sat up in bed and that's when she realized the state she was in. *Naked.* Lifting the covers, Morgan noted she still had on her underwear, but that didn't mean anything. Had she gotten it wrong? Had Jared done the unthinkable? She didn't feel any different. And wouldn't she? If they'd had sex, she would know. She was a virgin after all.

Yeah, the last of her kind, Morgan was sure. Most twenty-five-year-olds had had sex, but then again none of them had been raised by a mother like Crystal. But that was beside the point. If nothing happened between her and Jared, that meant he'd undressed her, seen her naked and left anyway. Morgan wanted to cheer in appreciation, but was also mortified to know after seeing her naked, it had done nothing for him. Then again, she doubted Jared wanted a corpse in bed.

Throwing back the covers, Morgan headed to the bathroom. As she brushed her teeth, she determined to look at the bright side. Jared was a good guy who'd saved her from a worse fate. Who knew what could have happened if he hadn't stepped in? When she was done, she wiped her mouth, turned on the taps for the shower and stepped in. She wanted the stench of last night off her.

She wasn't a heavy drinker. Or at least not usually. But yesterday was not ordinary. It wasn't every day the father you'd longed for your entire life rejected you. She had cause to drink, but Morgan vowed to never put herself in another situation like last night ever again.

When she was done, she turned off the shower and began toweling herself dry. In the closet, Morgan found her standard outfit of black jeans and a black T-shirt. She dressed like that every day to stay in the background as Dane's assistant. She was certain she wouldn't have a job for much longer once Dane found out what she'd done, but she was a college grad. Surely, she could find a new gig to pay the bills.

In the meantime, her role in Dane's life also gave her advantages because Morgan knew the Stewarts's schedule. They planned on leaving today to head back to Austin. She would have to go onto their turf to fight this battle. She wasn't going to cower and run off into the night like some poor relation. She was his *daughter* and Henry owed her. Owed her for all the missed birthday parties and Christmases. He owed her for not looking after her welfare and ensuring she had a happy, loving childhood.

And she was going to claim her due.

"Jared, are you listening to a word I've said?" his mother asked as he sat across the table where he and his parents were having Sunday brunch. It had been a weekly event ever since he was a kid. They hadn't stopped even after his father's heart attack and open-heart surgery a year ago.

"I'm sorry, Mom. What was that?" Jared asked. He'd been distracted the last week. He supposed it had something to do with a certain brunette he hadn't been able to forget. He'd been sleeping fitfully, tossing and turning thinking about the hazel-eyed beauty.

Jared wondered how she was faring. News of Morgan's relation to Dane had been leaked to the press and the story was splashed over the tabloids. Dane was on his honeymoon while Morgan had disappeared.

"I asked you if you knew where your brother, Chris was," Mary Robinson inquired. "It's not like him to miss Sunday brunch."

"No. I haven't talked to him," Jared answered. "His assistant said he took the week off for personal business."

"Chris is a workaholic, same as me," his father said. "I'm glad to see he's learned a lesson from me and is taking time for himself."

"What about Dane?" his mother asked. "I tried calling Nora about the tabloids' claim that Henry has an illegitimate daughter, but she didn't answer. Do you think it's true?"

"C'mon, Mary, you can't believe the gossips."

"It's not gossip, Dad," Jared replied.

His father frowned. "How would you know?"

"I met Morgan at the wedding. We talked and she's a lovely young woman."

"Who's no doubt after the Stewart wealth. She might be shocked to learn that not everything is what it seems. Henry hasn't been rolling in it for years," his father said. "If it wasn't for his son-in-law Gage and Fallon's business acumen, the company would have gone belly-up years ago."

"Not everything is about money," Jared said. "Morgan just wants to be recognized."

"So you're on a first name basis with her?" his mother asked, quirking a brow.

"You know our son can't resist a pretty face," his father responded. "She must be a looker."

Jared's spine stiffened at the affront and he wiped his mouth with his napkin. "I've lost my appetite, so I'll be on my way."

"Run away like you always do," his father countered.

"I'm sorry your favorite son couldn't be here for brunch, but don't take it out on me." Jared walked over to his mother and kissed her on the cheek. "Mom, I'll call you later."

Jared didn't bother saying goodbye to his father. They were never going to see eye to eye, so he'd stopped trying. He was curious about Morgan, but perhaps it was for the best he hadn't seen her since that night. He hadn't recognized himself around her and Jared suspected if he ever saw her again, he would be in trouble. He doubted he could walk away again.

Morgan sat in her car outside the Stewart mansion that afternoon. It had taken a week to get her affairs in order, which included starting the paperwork to legally change her name from Morgan Young to Morgan Stewart. It was time she took her rightful name and place in the family. She'd also sent a letter of resignation to Dane. Within days of the wedding, news had broken that she was Dane Stewart's baby sister and the tabloids were staked outside of her small apartment in Culver City. Thankfully, she'd packed in advance and decided to drive to Austin. Flying would have drawn too much attention. She lived frugally and Dane paid her well, so she had savings to tide her over for a while.

And now here she was, waiting for security to approve her entry to the hallowed grounds. Morgan fumed in her car. She was a Stewart, after all, and was being treated like she was an outsider. *But wasn't she?*

She hadn't been raised on this estate like Dane or Fallon. They'd had everything. The best house. Clothes. Cars. Education. While she'd had nothing. She had a right to be here. Henry was going to own up to being her father. Morgan wasn't going to leave until he did.

The security guard placed the receiver of his phone down and leaned out of the guardhouse. "I'm sorry, ma'am. I'm told you don't have an appointment. You're going to have to turn around."

"You can't keep me out," Morgan insisted. "I need to talk to my father."

"I'm sorry, miss. But you're going to have to leave. If you don't, I'm going to have to call the cops on you for trespassing."

"Trespassing?" Morgan's voice rose. "Well that's rich. Imagine what the press will say when they find out Henry kicked his own daughter off the grounds."

A horn sounded from behind Morgan and startled her. She turned as a red Audi pulled up beside her Honda Accord. The window rolled down and Fallon leaned out, but she wasn't alone. Ayden, their older brother, sat beside her. "It's all right, Drew. She's with me."

"Are you sure? Your father was insistent she not be let in."

"I'll handle my father," Fallon responded evenly. "Morgan—" Fallon glanced in her direction "—follow me in."

Morgan nodded mutely, put the car in gear and followed the Audi up the manicured road. When they finally stopped in front of the two-story mansion, Morgan sucked in a breath as she looked around.

After turning off the engine, Morgan exited the vehicle and found Fallon leaning against her car. She looked poised and sophisticated in jeans, a tank top, knee-high boots and a long duster. Morgan was sure the outfit was designer while her own was off-the-rack. Although Dane paid her well, living in Los Angeles was expensive and Morgan couldn't afford designer clothes.

Ayden, meanwhile, stood nearby, quietly assessing her. Morgan wished the situation was different and he would wrap her in a big brotherly hug. *Wasn't that what she'd always wanted?* A family of her own. Not just her and Crystal and the revolving door of men in her mother's life.

"Morgan, it seems we have a lot to talk about," Fallon said, her hazel eyes trained on Morgan. They were the same eyes Morgan saw every day when she looked in the mirror.

"No offense, Fallon, but *we* don't," Morgan said, folding her arms across her chest. "I need to talk to your father, I mean, *our* father."

"I disagree," Ayden said. "This involves all of us. Henry has a lot to answer for. It's why we both came. For answers."

"And I'm here to be a mediator," Fallon added. "I know neither of you is Daddy's biggest fan, but after your revelation last week, my mother was distraught.

Inconsolable. She came home with me and Gage and has been there all week. She asked me to bring a few things, which is why I'm here."

"I'm sorry," Morgan said, "but that's not my fault. I didn't cheat on her. Henry did."

"It wouldn't be the first time," Ayden said underneath his breath.

Fallon gave Ayden a hard stare. "That might be true, but surely you could have revealed your existence in a less public way?"

Morgan sighed. Fallon had a point. "I—I didn't know another way, Fallon. He didn't know me from Adam. I knew he would stonewall me. And as you can see from today, I was right."

"That's because he's hurt and lashing out."

"Do you always make excuses for him?" Morgan asked.

"Yes." Ayden nodded.

Fallon laughed. "I know Daddy isn't perfect."

"He's my father, too," Morgan responded hotly. "And it's time he acknowledged that."

"Let's go inside and talk. But I warn you he's not in the best mood."

Morgan followed Ayden and Fallon through the gilded doors with gold-plated handles into the foyer. She was amazed at how beautiful the mansion was. The terrazzo floors gleamed and the two-story spiral staircase was breathtaking. Morgan could see the European influence in the decor. It resembled a French chateau with cathedral ceilings and baroque adornments throughout. Fallon led Morgan into a sitting room that had a massive two-story fireplace and a baby grand piano.

Fallon sat down on a chaise and Ayden took the spot beside her. Morgan envied the easy comfort they shared and hoped one day she could have the same.

"Why do you think he's your father?" Fallon asked.

Morgan sighed. She didn't care to explain herself, but apparently she had to. "My mother met Henry when he was attending a tech convention in Las Vegas. They spent one night together. I'm the result. It's as simple as that."

"Why didn't she ever come forward? I mean, she could have gone to court and gotten my father to acknowledge you and pay child support. It's what I would've done."

"If you recall, my mother didn't fight to ensure Henry took care of me, either," Ayden interjected. "It's not easy coming forward."

"Thank you, Ayden." Morgan appreciated the backup considering their background was similar when it came to their father. "I doubt my mother knew how to find him. She said she didn't know who he was until a magazine article came out on Stewart Technologies, but she never told me until she was dying in the hospital."

"I'm so sorry," Fallon replied.

"It's all right. My mother and I didn't have a great relationship, which is why I wanted a father so badly."

"Then why didn't you tell us the truth sooner?" Fallon inquired. "You've been working for Dane for over a year."

"Fallon's right. We would have accepted you," Ayden said.

"I wanted to, but I was scared of how I would be received. Dane is a huge superstar. Considering his position, he might have thought I was trying to shake him down or something."

"Well, aren't you?" a harsh tenor voice sounded from behind them.

Morgan turned to see Henry. She didn't know how long he'd been standing there listening to their conversation.

Her father sauntered into the living room and Morgan felt his negativity from where she sat. It enshrouded him like a dark cloak. He looked foreboding even though he was dressed casually in navy trousers and a checkered button-down shirt. "You're here to claim what's yours? Isn't that right?"

"Daddy." Fallon rose to greet him. Morgan watched as Henry embraced his eldest daughter and accepted the kiss on her cheek, but his eyes never left Morgan's.

Morgan spoke quietly yet succinctly from the couch. "I'm here because it's time you acknowledge I'm your daughter."

"I don't know what lies your mama has been filling your head with, but I'm not your father."

"Prove it," Morgan stated. "Take a DNA test. If I'm wrong, which I don't think I am, I'll publicly admit I made the whole story up. But if I'm right—you have to claim me."

"*I* don't have to do a damn thing," Henry responded, moving toward her until he was inches away. "Who do you think you are? Steamrolling your way into our lives, into my home, and making demands?"

"Back off." Ayden jumped to his feet. Morgan appreciated that her big brother was ready to defend her from the big bad wolf, but she could fight her own battles.

"I'm—I'm your daughter." Morgan's voice broke. "How can you treat me this way?"

Fallon stepped between them and pushed her father backward. "Daddy, please…don't make this any worse. Do you have any idea how upset Mom is? I know you're no saint, but admit what you did. Maybe she can forgive you, but if you continue to act as if nothing happened—" she glanced at Morgan "—you're going to dig yourself deeper into a hole."

"Fallon, I appreciate what you're trying to do, but my relationship with Nora is mine alone. I don't need your interference."

"I think you do," Fallon responded hotly. "Look at her!" Once again, Fallon's gaze rested on Morgan. "She has our same eyes, Daddy. I'm surprised I never saw it before, but I suppose I wasn't looking."

"Admit it, Henry!" Ayden snarled. "You cheated on Nora. Just like you did my mother. Be a man about it and own up to what you've done!"

Henry walked up to Ayden. And Morgan thought if looks could kill, both men would have been struck dead in an instant. "Don't get in the middle of this, Ayden, and start stirring up the past. We've come to a truce. Let sleeping dogs lie, son."

Ayden shook his head. "I won't let you deny another child. Not this time and not on my watch."

"Why are you both ganging up on me?" Henry asked, looking at Ayden and Fallon. "Isn't it enough my marriage is in shambles because of this girl?"

"This girl?" Tears sprang to Morgan's eyes. "This girl grew up poor with nothing to call my own. No friends. We moved from pillar to post as my mother tried to find work, but it's not easy for an aging Vegas showgirl to

find work. She turned to men, hoping they'd take care of her. There was an endless stream of them in and out of her life. In and out of *my* life. So I never had a father, much less a home. And when the men were gone, the drugs started—until eventually her body gave out from the drug use."

"I'm sorry for your childhood. Truly I am, but I owe you nothing. And if either of you—" Henry glanced at his other children "—are with her, then you can show yourselves out because I'm done with this conversation."

Morgan watched in astonishment as the father she'd hoped would acknowledge her walked out of the room. Morgan pulled the knife out of her heart and stood ramrod straight.

"Wow! I can't believe the nerve of that man." Ayden scrubbed the stubble on his jaw. "Just when I think he can't sink any lower, he proves me wrong."

"I have to go." Morgan started toward the exit.

"Wait!" Fallon reached for her arm. "Don't go. Give me some time to talk to him. I can get through to him."

Ayden nodded. "If anyone can, it's Fallon. She's his favorite."

"Ayden…" Fallon glared at him.

He held up his hands in mock surrender.

"Please stay," Fallon said softly. "We can figure this out. *As a family.*"

Morgan snorted. "Didn't you hear him?" She pointed at the empty doorway. "I'm not your family. I'm a nothing. A nobody. So leave me be. I want no part of any of you!" She wrenched her arm away and ran out.

When she got in the car, Morgan was hyperventilating and tears were streaming down her cheeks. She slammed her fists against the steering wheel.

Damn him!

Why had she let him get to her? She had been determined to be strong and demand what was rightfully hers, but instead Henry Stewart made it obvious he had no intention of recognizing her as his daughter. Instead, he was going to keep his head in the sand and act as if she didn't exist.

Morgan was done with being nice. She was going to the press with her story and give the press an exposé on the great Henry Stewart. She wouldn't allow him to ignore her ever again.

Four

"I need to see you right away," Ruth Robinson told Jared later that evening.

Jared rarely received a summons from his grandmother. In fact, he tried to stay off her radar. Similar to his father, his grandmother wished he was more like his brother. Chris was the smart one with the brains and business acumen to run Robinson Holdings. Chris had never caused their parents a moment's worry. He did exactly what was expected of him. Attend Harvard. Check. Attain an MBA. Join Robinson Holdings. Check. Check.

Jared, on the other hand, was the screwup. He'd attained his bachelor's degree in marketing by the skin of his teeth. He'd been too busy partying it up with his fraternity brothers of Kappa Alpha Psi and taking the ladies to bed to bother with classes. After graduation, he'd taken a year off to travel Europe and then returned home to work at the family business.

After driving through the hills of Westlake overlooking Austin's skyline, Jared pulled his Porsche Cayman GTS through the gates of his grandmother's estate and parked. The grounds were kept immaculate by her staff and the house was nothing short of castle-like.

Stepping out of the car, he walked the short distance to the front door and rang the doorbell. A uniformed butler greeted him. "Hey, Antoine." He patted the older man's back as he entered the sprawling home. Antoine had been with his grandmother for years and was devoted to her. "Where's Grandmother?"

"In the library," Antoine replied. "Allow me to show you there."

"No need to stand on ceremony. Go back to whatever you were doing. I can find my way." Jared strolled down the Italian marble corridor until he found his grandmother in the mahogany-paneled library seated in a gold leaf armchair.

"Well, look who finally decided to make an appearance." She rose to her feet as he walked over and placed a kiss on her cheek.

Ruth Robinson was nothing short of regal with smooth café au lait skin and expert makeup. Even at seventy-five, she looked amazing in a crisp white shirt with billowing sleeves, black slacks and pearls. Her blondish gray hair was in an elegant coiffed bob that reached her shoulders.

"Grandma, it's good to see you too," Jared replied. "Would you care for a drink?"

"Would love one."

Jared crossed the room to a small bar tucked in the

corner. He poured himself a Scotch and a sherry for her, then brought her the glass and settled on a plush tan leather sofa. He leaned back and took a swallow of his drink.

His grandmother sipped her sherry and looked him directly in the eye. "You're going to have to learn the value of time once this scandal hits."

Jared sat upright at her comment. "What are you talking about?"

"Mimi, a dear friend of mine who owns one of the Austin newspapers, gave me a call about an exclusive story hitting their paper tomorrow."

"Oh yeah? What's it about?" Jared brought his tumbler to his lips.

"Your brother knocking up an exotic dancer," Ruth stated unceremoniously.

Jared's drink sputtered from his lips. "Excuse me?"

"For Christ's sake, Jared." His grandmother rolled her eyes. "Clean yourself up."

Jared jumped to his feet, swiftly walked to the bar and grabbed several napkins, then dabbed at his shirt. When he was finished, he returned to stand in front of his grandmother.

"Sit."

Jared didn't argue and sat down. "I don't understand."

"What I've told you is as much as I know," she responded. "Chris has been MIA from Robinson Holdings the last week. He must have known the story was coming. But the worst part is he got the young woman pregnant. It's a travesty. I had such high hopes for your brother, but I guess that leaves you." Her eyes rested on him and Jared shifted uncomfortably in his seat.

"What's that supposed to mean?"

"Chris has shown poor judgment. If he can't manage his own love life, how can he be expected to run a billion-dollar real estate company? The answer is simple. He can't."

"Yes, he can," Jared replied. "So what he got a girl pregnant? It happens. It's not the end of the world. You're making too much of this."

"I disagree. Your grandfather and I worked too hard building up the business and our image as respectable stewards for our investors. We can't allow your brother's bad behavior to negatively impact the company. He's out. And you're in."

"Me?" Jared couldn't contain the disbelief in his tone. "You've got to be kidding. Chris has been groomed to run the company. He's your man. Furthermore, I'm not interested." He tipped back his glass, finished his drink and placed it on the cocktail table in front of him and stood.

"Sit down." His grandmother's voice rose.

"Grandma..."

"I said, sit down, Jared. I won't repeat myself."

Jared sighed, but did as she instructed. "I'm not cut out for this. I don't know the first thing about running the company. I'm in marketing."

"With the right people behind you, you'll learn."

"No." Jared shook his head and pursed his lips. "I can't do it."

"You can and you will." His grandmother stated unequivocally, dismissing his protest. "For too long, we've allowed you to monkey about, but no more. You will pick up the mantel like your father and brother before you."

Jared hated being pushed into a corner and he certainly didn't relish going up against the matriarch of their family, but what she was asking was ridiculous.

"You will start tomorrow." Ruth spoke as if Jared's taking Chris's place was a foregone conclusion. "I've taken the liberty of requesting the files on Chris's current acquisitions." She rose to her feet and went to a side table containing a stack of files. She handed them to Jared. "Read them over tonight and we'll talk in the morning."

He stared at her incredulously. "You're serious about this?"

"Of course. You should know me well enough to know when I make up my mind, it's done."

Jared did know and that was exactly what he was afraid of. He wasn't cut out to run Robinson Holdings. He was good at being a ladies' man and working when he felt like it, but *this*, *this* was too much. And he had no idea how to get out of it. God help them, because the business and their family were in for a bumpy ride.

When Jared made it to his penthouse after leaving his grandmother's, his first call was to Chris. But it went straight to voice mail.

What was going on?

Chris's silence was unusual. He never ignored Jared's calls—usually because he was bailing Jared out of a mess of his own creation. But this was different. On his way home, Jared stopped by Chris's usual spots—the gym, the office, a gentleman's club he sometimes frequented—but nothing. Chris didn't want to be found.

Jared couldn't understand his brother giving away

everything he'd worked so hard to earn. For what? A woman? They were interchangeable at best or had always been for Jared. He had never met a woman who made him want to risk it all for love. Because that's exactly what Chris was doing. Their grandmother was ready to disinherit him for this stunt.

But this time, Jared was left holding the bag. Was this what it felt like when Jared went MIA after causing trouble? Now that the shoe was on the other foot, Jared was not pleased. He was used to Chris saving the day, but his grandmother was looking to *him*.

The responsibility she was putting on his shoulders was heavy and Jared felt the weight. He felt unsure. Unworthy. *How could he ever live up to Chris?* He couldn't. He would have to prove his worth until he earned his grandmother's respect, but it wouldn't be easy. The question was whether he was up to the task.

Morgan curled up on the sofa in her hotel room with a tub of Ben & Jerry's ice cream she'd picked up on her way back from the Stewart estate. She'd already consumed half a pizza and two beers and was doing her best to eat herself through her troubles.

The last week hadn't been stellar. The only bright spot had been seeing Dane and Iris get married and ride off into the sunset. Maybe she'd been wrong in approaching Henry after the reception, but she'd thought confronting him in public would force his hand. Make him own up to the truth that he'd cheated on Nora and had a child with another woman.

Morgan hadn't banked on Henry's temper. Or that he would completely shut her out and refuse to acknowledge her existence. Even when confronted by his own children, who begged for the truth, Henry refused to admit it.

Maybe she was better off not having a father?

None of the men her mother ever brought into her life had been father material. They were interested in using Crystal only for their own pleasure. Morgan hated seeing her mother dependent on them and so desperate for attention she'd take it from anyone. Including *him*.

Morgan sank her spoon into the chunky mixture and kept eating as she recalled one of those men. Troy Wilkins had been one of her mother's boyfriends. Often, he'd stay the night and when he did, Morgan locked her bedroom door. She'd hated him on sight. He was lean and wiry with ominous-looking eyes that were always roving over her. Morgan tried to steer clear, but one day when she'd come home from high school, he'd been at their apartment. Troy told her Crystal had gone to the grocery store.

Immediately Morgan invented an excuse and tried to make a quick exit, but Troy was faster than her. He'd slammed the front door and put the chain across, locking her inside with him. Morgan had been terrified and rightfully so. Troy told her it was time she was friendlier to him and had grabbed her by the arm and hauled Morgan into her bedroom.

He'd thrown her on the bed and covered her with his weight before she could move. She remembered the stale scent of cigarettes permeating his skin, the smell of alcohol on his breath. Then he was lifting her shirt up, palming her small breasts and rubbing his crotch against her. Morgan tried to fight him off, knowing if she didn't, he would assault her, but he was too strong. His hands were reaching for the snap on her jeans when they both heard the door. Her mother was calling out to them.

"If you tell your mother, I'll deny this ever happened. Who do you think she'll believe?"

Morgan would never forget the look in his eye. That was when she'd known she couldn't stay there. She'd had to get out. If she didn't, he'd come back and there would be no guarantee she'd be as lucky the next time. And so she'd run. She'd packed her meager belongings and left. She'd gone to her mom's friend Marilyn, another dancer, and begged to sleep on her couch. Even though Marilyn had two kids of her own, it was better than living in fear.

Marilyn allowed Morgan to stay on the sofa so long as she cooked, cleaned and tended her two kids while Marilyn worked nights as a dancer. Morgan happily agreed. The funny thing about it was—Crystal hadn't cared. She seemed happy to be rid of Morgan because she was cramping her style.

Somehow Morgan found a way to finish her senior year. Due to her good grades, she'd been able to attend the University of Southern California on a full scholarship.

When she thought about it, all her struggles were because both her parents refused to do right by her.

Morgan put down her ice cream on the cocktail table and reached for her iPad. Searching the web, she found the email for a local gossip blogger in Austin.

It was time one of her parents—Henry Stewart— paid the price.

Five

Jared, your father can't come back. His health is still too tenuous.

Monday morning, as the elevator zoomed up to the top floor of the office building where Robinson Holdings was housed, Jared thought about his mother's words from last night.

You're going to have to put on your big boy pants and do what needs to be done, his father had said.

Jared rolled his eyes as he thought about his father's condescending tone. He knew what a huge task it would be stepping into Chris's shoes. But there didn't seem to be anyone else to fill the role.

When the elevator chimed on the top floor, Jared exited wearing one of the many custom suits in his wardrobe. This time, however, he looked at everyone with new eyes. Instead of traipsing to his office for a few hours, he would be the decision maker. Many of these people depended on him. It was a scary position.

When he opened his office door, he was surprised to find his grandmother. She was dressed elegantly in a blazer over a silk shirt and trousers. "Grandmother, I didn't expect you."

She smiled, which was a rarity. "Since Clay's health precludes him from being here and your wayward brother is off with some dancer, I'm here to give you some reinforcement."

"I thought you've been retired from the business for years."

"I'm still on the board and come in from time to time. Keeps the mind strong and a woman of my age young."

"You don't look a day over fifty."

"No need to charm me, Jared. Leave that to the ladies whose hearts you have strewn across Austin."

Jared clutched his chest with one hand. "Grandma, you wound me."

"There's a board of director's meeting in an hour," Ruth said sternly. "Let's get down to business."

Two hours later, Jared already wanted to throw in the towel. The board of directors meeting had been a free-for-all with many speculating about what would happen to the company now that their CEO had vanished for parts unknown. Then his grandmother dropped the bombshell that *Jared* was taking over as CEO in Chris's absence. Many of the directors revolted. Some outright laughed and thought it was a joke.

"Jared doesn't know the first thing about running

this billion-dollar enterprise. He's about fast cars and women," one of the older board of directors scoffed.

"Jared may be green around the gills," Ruth responded evenly, "but listen when I say this. A *Robinson* will always run Robinson Holdings." Then she'd thrown them all for a loop when she'd said, "I'll be onsite in an advisory capacity to assist."

"You're putting the company at risk," another board member commented.

"I took a risk when I hired you, didn't I?" his grandmother replied.

After that, the meeting had continued smoothly with Ruth steering the ship. Now they were back in his office talking next steps over coffee.

"As head of the company, you'll need to keep your head low and avoid scandal. I don't want a repeat of what happened with your brother."

"I'm not Chris." Jared kept his affairs discreet.

"Good. Because as you can see, the board is looking for leadership. Your reputation as a ladies' man is well-known, which is why I think it's time you found a wife."

"I'm not ready for marriage, Grandmother. That's not in the cards for me. Maybe in the future, but not now."

She ignored him. "It would go a long way with the board embracing your leadership if you were settled."

"Don't you mean it would make you feel better?"

"Same difference."

"Well, you needn't worry because I already have a girlfriend." *Jeez. What possessed him to say that?* Jared knew why. He was sick and tired of being compared to Chris. Although he loved his brother, he wasn't incompetent.

His grandmother's large brown eyes grew wide in amazement. "Why is this the first I'm hearing about her?"

"Because it's new," Jared continued with the lie. *What choice did he have?* He'd already put his foot in his mouth. "And the press are always scrutinizing me, so we've kept our relationship private."

"I would like to meet her."

"It's too soon, Grandmother."

"Rubbish. You'll bring her over and introduce me." Ruth pulled a file out of the many stacked on his desk. "Let's get to work. You have a lunch meeting with a potential client Chris has been wooing and you need to be prepared."

His grandmother might consider the matter closed, but Jared certainly didn't. He didn't have a girlfriend. Nor did he have any prospects. Most of the women in his phone were of the affair variety. They were not the kind of women you brought home to meet your grandma. He was going to have to do some fancy footwork because he needed a fake girlfriend pronto!

Morgan felt confident as she drove to the posh restaurant where she was meeting the blogger Ally Peters. She told herself she was doing the right thing. By exposing Henry Stewart as her father, he would no longer be able to hide. He would be forced to face the truth and confront the allegations. *Could he ignore them?* There was always that possibility. But from the little she'd heard about Nora Stewart, she was *all* about reputation. She wouldn't abide having her family's name smeared in the mud. So one way or another the truth would come out and Morgan would be vindicated.

But at what cost? an inner voice asked. Last night, Morgan had received calls and texts from Fallon and Ayden respectively. Both of them had offered olive branches and wanted to talk, but the time for talking was over. It was time for action. The press was already speculating about whether her story was true. Since Morgan rarely had her picture taken and wasn't on social media, they couldn't find a recent photo. She was thankful for some anonymity.

Morgan pulled her Honda up to the valet and hopped out. She'd dressed smartly for her lunch in a sophisticated striped dress that hit at the thigh along with some knee-high boots and her favorite fedora hat.

"I have a reservation with Ally Peters?" Morgan told the hostess.

"Right this way." The statuesque blonde led her to a curved booth where the online gossip columnist was already seated. Her blog was extremely popular and had over two million followers.

"Morgan?" When she nodded, the redhead stood and air-kissed her. "Please have a seat. I already ordered some club soda. Hope you don't mind?"

"No, that's fine."

"I'm so excited to hear you dish." Ally rubbed her hands together with glee and a smile spread across her heart-shaped face. "You said you had a big reveal about a wealthy family here in Austin?"

"I do," Morgan said, but stopped herself as the waitress appeared. After ordering a peach sangria, Morgan continued. "I'm hoping you can get the truth out there because I feel as if I've been silenced."

"I hear you, girlfriend. And I've got an ear to listen."

Morgan was leaning her head toward Ally when a familiar voice from a table several feet away stopped her cold. *It couldn't be.* They'd met only once, but Morgan was certain she'd never forget the voice of the man she'd nearly gone to bed with. When he turned his head, Morgan caught sight of him.

Jared.

Morgan sucked in a deep breath. She would recognize that tall drink of water anywhere. Those bedroom eyes. The full, thick lips that had kissed her until sensations coursed through her, electrifying her entire being.

"Morgan, you were saying?" Ally interrupted her musings to bring her back to their conversation, but Morgan's brain was mush.

Morgan couldn't stop staring at Jared or pull her gaze away from his mouth, remembering how he'd plundered hers with it. Her mind was spinning. She never thought she'd see Jared again. *What were the odds they'd ever run into each other again?* It had to be fate or kismet or something.

Then Jared looked up and their eyes connected from across the room. His gaze held hers in a searing tether, causing a shiver to run down Morgan's spine. His pupils were black and bottomless pools of ink and Morgan felt her cheeks getting hot. She blinked and broke the stare.

"Who are you ogling?" Ally turned to look across the room. Then she spun back around with a wide grin on her mouth. "Is something going on between you and Jared? Omigod, it would be sooo delicious. This morning, the newspapers had a story about his brother, Chris, running off with some stripper. And now this…"

"*This* is nothing," Morgan said quickly—too quickly because Ally's brow rose. "I was merely looking at an attractive man."

"And he was staring right back at you. There's a story there."

"You're mistaken. My story is about the..."

Morgan didn't get to finish her statement because suddenly Jared was standing at their table. He looked as he had the night of the wedding, except today he was in a gray suit with a blue-and-white-striped tie. He was every bit the corporate tycoon, which she wouldn't have guessed him to be.

"Morgan." Jared looked at her, ignoring Ally, who was positively giddy.

"Jared."

"I see my timing is immaculate," he said, not taking his eyes off Morgan. "Mind if I sit down?" He didn't wait for an answer and immediately sat across from Morgan.

"No, not at all." Ally spoke since Morgan was tongue-tied at seeing the sexy stranger she'd fantasized about in the flesh.

"What are you doing, Morgan?" Jared inquired, staring at her.

"Ally and I were chatting about a big story I have."

His frown went deep as he peered at her intently. "Do you really think that's wise?"

"It's none of your business," Morgan stated hotly. "If I recall, you don't want to be a knight in shining armor."

His eyes darkened and sexual energy crackled in the air like static electricity. When Morgan ran her tongue over her suddenly dry lips, his eyes dropped to her mouth and then quickly jerked back to her eyes as if he were fighting some inner demon.

Jared looked at the other occupant of the booth. "Ally, would you mind if she rescheduled your meeting?"

"No, I..." Morgan tried in vain to talk, but one withering look from Jared cut her sentence short.

"Of course I don't mind." Ally slid out of the booth and gathered her purse and tablet. Morgan knew the gossip columnist was conjuring all sorts of juicy gossip about Jared and Morgan. Not Henry Stewart.

Jared was ruining everything. Why did *he* have to be here today?

Ally reached inside her purse and pulled out a business card, but instead of handing it to Morgan, who'd been the one to call her, Ally handed it to Jared. "Give me a call. I'd love to talk to you more." She gave him a wink and seconds later was walking out of the restaurant.

Morgan fumed in her seat. "How dare you?"

She didn't get another word out before Jared was beside her, sliding his hand behind her neck and bringing his mouth down on hers.

Jared had no self-control when it came to this woman. When he saw Morgan sitting with Ally, a notorious gossip blogger, his heart slammed against his chest. He'd known what she was about to do. Blow her life up. *He had to stop her.* Kissing her had been the last thing on his agenda, but now that he'd started, he didn't want the kiss to end. He could kiss her all day and all night.

He relished Morgan's fruity taste from the cocktail she'd been drinking. Her lips were soft and pillowy and clung to his. When his tongue darted inside to meet hers, they danced together, making his pulse throb. But they were in public, so Jared pulled back.

Morgan stared at him wide-eyed, her mouth slightly swollen and her cheeks flushed. "Did you kiss me to shut me up?"

Jared grinned. "Maybe. Did it work?"

Morgan chewed her lip and Jared could feel his erection press against his zipper. "You know it did, but stopping me from going after Ally won't prevent the inevitable. I intend to have my say."

"To what end?" Jared inquired. "It won't make Henry accept you. In fact, he and the other Stewarts might resent you for the negative press you're heaping on them. Did you think about that? And what about Dane, your brother?"

"When he gets back, he'll find I've tendered my resignation. I can't continue working for him after all that's happened."

"I think that's a mistake because Dane will want to get to know you, but regardless, don't you think he's been through enough in the media the last year without you dredging up more family secrets?"

Morgan was silent. He hoped she was listening to what he said. The press had been all over Dane when the story broke about him falling in love with Iris, the woman who'd used his anonymous sperm donation to become pregnant. Having their romance heavily televised had come at a price. He didn't want that for his friend or Morgan again.

"What do you expect me to do?" Morgan finally choked out.

"Be patient. And listen to me. I'm trying to save you from yourself."

"I don't need saving."

"Might I remind you of the stunts you pulled at the wedding? Your big revelation. Getting drunk. Attempting to spend the night with a complete stranger."

"You're not a stranger anymore," Morgan responded. "I know your full name now. Jared Robinson."

Jared couldn't resist smiling. "Yes, you do."

"So tell me, Mr. Robinson, why did you leave without…?"

"Without making love to you?" Jared offered. Because he'd wanted to. *Badly.* He'd wanted to caress every inch of her body and take her to heights of profound pleasure. Making love to Morgan would have been very satisfying. His loins had throbbed for days from unrequited lust, but he'd also wanted Morgan to remember him in the morning and not regret her actions.

Morgan flushed, clearly embarrassed at his directness. But then she surprised him, by glancing up at him underneath her lashes. "Why? Any other man might have taken advantage."

"I'm not any other man."

"No, you're not."

"I'm glad. And I'm going to continue being a man of mystery by offering you a deal you can't refuse."

"And what's that?"

"I need a girlfriend. A very public one and I've decided you're great for the role. So how about it?"

Six

Morgan threw back her head and let out an uproarious laugh. It was a reflexive response because she didn't know what to make of Jared Robinson. Sometimes he was the sexy stranger she'd met at a wedding. Other times he was a white knight trying to save her. He kept her off-kilter and she couldn't figure him out.

Jared frowned. "What's so funny?"

"You were joking, right?" Morgan asked when her laughter subsided.

"No, I'm not."

Jared's expression was somber and Morgan realized she'd miscalculated. "You're serious? You want me to be your girlfriend? But why? According to Ally, you're quite the ladies' man. Stands to reason you don't need a girl like me."

"I may not *need* a girl like you, but you're the girl I *want*," Jared declared.

Morgan's heart went pitter pat. Wasn't it enough she felt as if he'd permanently branded her with his steaming-hot kiss? Her lips were still tingling from the searing heat of his mouth. His kiss had literally awakened her body to what was possible.

"Why?"

"I would think it's obvious. You're a beautiful woman and I'm attracted to you, Morgan. And if I'm not mistaken, the feeling is mutual. We could enjoy each other's company while you help me with my image problem."

"And why is your image important right now?"

"My brother, Chris, who was running the family business, has vanished with an exotic dancer. He left without a trace, causing a vacuum in leadership. My family and board of directors are looking to me to fill that void. Considering my dubious reputation, it might be an easier pill for them to swallow if I was a bit more...*settled*."

"In a committed relationship?"

He pointed with his index finger at her. "There you have it. Having a girlfriend would ease their concerns about my former status as a ladies' man."

"And what would be in it for me?"

A sexy grin spread across his full lips. "Time spent in my sparkling company and I'm a pretty good date if I do say so myself. And if you were my girlfriend, you'd want for nothing. And as a bonus, you can have the family you've always wanted—*mine*—for a limited period. Once the board is settled, we end our association."

"Your suggestion is a win-win for you," Morgan replied, reaching for her sangria and taking a sip. "As much as I love the offer of spending time with you and borrowing your family, I'm going to have to decline."

"Why? Do you have somewhere else pressing to be? Or perhaps a significant other I'm not aware of?"

Morgan laughed. As if. She'd never had a boyfriend because she'd never allowed anyone to get close enough to become one. Her near assault had frightened her from getting involved with men. In college, she'd watched her roommates and other friends falling in and out of love, but it hadn't happened for her. Morgan feared something was wrong with her. Until Jared. Until the night when she'd made out with a stranger.

"Well?"

Morgan realized he was still waiting for her to respond to his questions. "There's no one else."

Did his shoulders visibly relax? Morgan wondered. Or was she projecting? "Then why not?"

"Because I'm still trying to figure out my place in life. It may not be with the Stewarts, but it's not with you, either."

"Fair enough. But didn't you say you've given your notice to Dane? That means you're unemployed for the moment, so why not stay here in Austin for a spell. Afterward, when we go our separate ways I could help you. I have lots of connections. I can help you attain whatever future you desire. So tell me, what's it going to take to convince you to agree?"

Morgan allowed herself a swift glance underneath her lashes at Jared. She let her eyes linger on the sculpted planes of his face and his exceptionally firm and square chin. The impeccable cut of Jared's suit and his indefinable aura of wealth were entrancing. Morgan felt hypnotized. *Was that why she was starting to give his offer serious consideration?* Was she really going to throw all her common sense away and plunge herself into the thrill of the unknown?

No, she had to think logically. Tearing away her gaze from his for a moment, she looked down. It was easy for him to make her such an outrageous offer because in his world women were ornaments he could discard when he was done with them. If she did this, Morgan would have to ensure she was in a better position when it was over than when they began. Because there was no assurance Henry would ever accept her into the Stewart family, which meant she was on her own. Since she'd tendered her resignation to Dane, she would need a job and she didn't want any help from her brother.

"I want a job at a network or production company," Morgan stated. Film was in her blood. "I've been working for Dane over the last year and I've learned a lot. Not to mention the degree I have. An MFA in screenwriting."

"I'll make it happen," Jared replied. "So can I consider you my girlfriend now?"

"Yes. Should we shake on it?"

"I have a better idea."

As he slid closer to her in the booth, understanding dawned on her. Morgan tilted her head back a little as he slowly came toward her. Lifting his hand to cup her face, he dipped his head and closed his mouth over hers.

Jared had to kiss her again. Morgan was so sweet and honest. He appreciated her directness. It was a huge turn-on. And so he kissed her with all the passion and longing he'd tried to clamp down but couldn't. Morgan clutched the lapels of his suit while she pressed her soft trembling lips to his, which told Jared she was as much a slave to their passion as he was. Slowly, he straightened and looked at her.

Her hazel-gray eyes shimmered with desire and made Jared's groin tighten in response. "It's settled then. You're mine."

His possessive tone must have snapped Morgan out of her passion-induced gaze because she replied, "I'm not yours or anybody's. I'm my own person. But I will help you and in return you'll help me get my dream job."

"Yes of course." Jared stared at her luminous eyes fringed with long black lashes and imagined her thick and lustrous black hair spread out on a pillow as he feasted on her.

Morgan may not have been his usual type. In the looks department, yes, but he found her too unguarded. She was unlike his typical lovers who were sleek and sophisticated. They welcomed him into their beds because of his name and rumored prowess. But she had an air of innocence, which told him that night in La Jolla was a fluke.

"So what do I need to do first?"

"Convince my grandmother Ruth that our relationship is legit."

Morgan smiled. "How hard can it be to convince a sweet old lady we're a couple?"

Jared snorted. "You don't know my grandmother. The woman is a force to be reckoned with. She helped my grandfather build the company."

"She sounds like an amazing woman."

"She is. And very astute," he responded. "We need to be on top of our game if we're going to convince her, which means we should probably spend some time getting to know each other. Otherwise, she'll sense something isn't right."

Morgan leaned back in the booth. "Considering I'm unemployed, my schedule is pretty open."

He reached inside his jacket pocket and produced his iPhone. "Good. What's your phone number?" She told him and he punched in her digits. "I have to get to a meeting, but I'll be in touch." He rose to his feet and buttoned his suit jacket. "We'll make a good team, you and me."

He turned away and strode out of the restaurant. He had to. Morgan was temptation personified and he could easily get distracted trying to seduce her. Jared would have to ensure they weren't alone together often. Otherwise, he was certain this arrangement of theirs would end with the two of them wrapped in each other's arms to the exclusion of everything else.

Had she really just agreed to be Jared's pretend girl-friend? Morgan thought as she walked through the revolving doors of her hotel that afternoon. *And exactly what did that entail?* They hadn't gone over the details or his expectations other than that he would take care of her. Did that mean he was going to take care of her hotel bill?

Not long after she'd settled in her room, she heard a knock. She wasn't expecting anyone. Padding to the door barefoot, she glanced through the peephole and was surprised to see Ayden on the other side. "Please open up. I'd like to talk."

Morgan swung open the door. "Why would you want to talk to me when I've been ignoring you?"

Ayden swept past her into the room without an invitation. "Because you're my sister."

Morgan closed the door and turned around to face him. She folded her arms across her chest and regarded him. Her brother was handsome. In slacks and button-down shirt, he looked like their father. "So you believe me?"

Ayden's brow furrowed. "Of course I do. I don't doubt Henry was capable of cheating on Nora like he did my mother."

"Thank you." She walked over to the small sitting area and sat down. Ayden joined her.

"Years ago, I promised Fallon I'd be a better big brother," Ayden began. "I'm here today to be that brother. You got a raw deal."

Morgan couldn't resist a small smile. She didn't want to like him, but she did. "Ayden…"

"Regardless of whether our father says you're his daughter, you're my sister."

"Why won't he admit the truth?" Morgan asked softly.

Ayden shrugged. "Pride? I can tell you Henry isn't any easy man to like, let alone love."

"How did you forgive him after everything he did to you?" Morgan knew Ayden's story. Henry had divorced his mother, Lillian, to marry Nora, the woman he'd cheated on her with. He gave Lillian a small settlement and never acknowledged Ayden as his first-born until recently.

"I haven't," Ayden responded. "I've learned to accept the things I cannot change and keep peace for the family, but I haven't forgotten. Because as he has with you, Henry has never admitted he did anything wrong."

"I don't know if I can let this go."

"And if Henry doesn't ever accept you, what then? You have to move on with your life, Morgan. No good can come from you spending your life waiting for something that may never happen. Trust me, I know."

"I appreciate that you came to offer your support. It means a lot to me."

"Fallon would have joined me, but Dylan has a stomach bug and she's at home with him. Both of us—and I'm sure Dane—will be by your side."

"Have you heard from him?"

Ayden shook his head. "I don't expect to, after such a harrowing six months. Dane and Iris wanted to be off the radar for a few weeks. Her parents are taking care of Jayden." He reached for her hand across the short distance. "Dane may be upset with you at first, but he'll accept you just like me and Fallon."

Morgan's mouth lifted in a smile. "You're pretty good at this big brother thing."

"I've had some practice." Ayden stood. "I'll get out of your hair, but if you need anything I'm here for you." He leaned down and enveloped her in a warm hug Morgan hadn't known she'd needed.

A lump formed in her throat when he moved away. It was nice to finally have someone in *her* corner. "We'll talk soon, okay, kid?" Ayden stroked her cheek and then he was gone.

Ayden knew what it was like to walk in her shoes. Yet, he'd gone on to become successful and start Stewart Investments. *Was he right?* Should she let the desire to be acknowledged by their father go? Morgan wasn't sure she could, but she would try.

Seven

Jared surprised his grandmother and the board the rest of the week by working twelve-hour days and immersing himself in Robinson Holdings. He knew the business deals in progress or he wouldn't have been able to handle the marketing campaigns, but he'd never been involved in the development stage or seeing a project from beginning to end.

With Ruth's guidance, he was learning about everything firsthand. There was excitement blended with fear, but it bolstered his confidence when he saw respect in the eyes of his peers. Jared wasn't coasting like he usually did. He was digging in and finding he actually enjoyed what he was doing.

When the end of the day came on Friday, it shocked Jared to realize the week had gone by without him contacting Morgan. He felt like a heel for abandoning her when he'd been the one to suggest she become his pretend girlfriend. But he would make good on his promise.

Glancing at his Rolex, Jared saw it was almost dinnertime. It would be nice to spend the evening with a beautiful woman. His grandmother would notice if anything was amiss so he needed to ensure that he and Morgan were on solid footing. He reached for his phone and dialed her cell.

"So you didn't forget about me?" Morgan asked when she picked up.

"Forget you? As if that were possible," Jared said smoothly. "But in all seriousness, it's been a busy week here. My brother had a lot of pans in the fire, so I've been getting up to speed. Are you free for dinner? I was hoping we could grab a bite at my favorite spot."

"Sure. What time?"

"I can pick you up in an hour."

"That's okay. I can meet you there. What's the address?"

Why did she have to be obstinate? "No woman of mine would drive herself," Jared responded. "I would be expected to pick you up, so I'll see you at seven."

"Fine."

He smiled after Morgan gave him her hotel information. Morgan was getting the hang of it. He always got his way.

When Morgan opened the door, she prayed her makeup and hair piled atop her head looked flawless because Jared stood in her doorway looking every bit the man of power. He was stylish and polished in a tailored suit that showed off the broadness of his shoulders. He smiled, and his dimples and deliciously full lips were irresistible.

He was sexy. Too damn sexy.

Morgan's heart swelled and her pulse quickened when his eyes roved over her figure. "I hope what I'm wearing is okay. You didn't tell me the attire."

"You, um…look good." His voice sounded strangled.

"Good?" She pouted. "I was hoping for a better adjective."

Jared cleared his throat and his eyes moved slowly over her curves in the sleek strapless black dress. A muscle tightened in his jaw. "How about hot."

She glanced up at him and their eyes locked, causing her belly to flutter. "I'll take that." She stepped into the corridor, closing the door behind her because no way was she allowing him inside. He was looking at her like she was dessert.

Jared walked beside her, his hand lightly resting on the small of her back as they made their way to the elevator. It wasn't anything untoward; instead, it caused Morgan to feel safe.

After a short elevator ride, they disembarked in the lobby. Morgan was surprised when Jared laced his fingers with hers. Only when he'd settled her in the passenger seat of his Porsche did Morgan exhale.

She reminded herself this date was pretend. It wasn't real. Jared didn't want her. He needed a girlfriend to convince his grandmother he was a reformed playboy, but that didn't stop her womanly bits from wanting it to mean more.

* * *

The restaurant and jazz bar Jared took Morgan to wasn't the flashy place she'd expected. She'd assumed he would take her someplace the local celebrities went to so they could be "seen."

"What's wrong?" Jared asked when they were seated at a secluded table for two by the owner. "Don't you like the restaurant? They have a great jazz quartet and singer."

Morgan smiled. "I love it. I just didn't think you would."

"You think I'm bourgie?"

She laughed. "There's nothing wrong with being used to the finer things in life. It's how you were raised."

"I also appreciate simple, good food," Jared countered, looking down at his menu.

"I've offended you," Morgan said, frowning. "I'm sorry if I made an assumption. It's just you're *you* and I thought you'd want us to be seen, which is why I wore this dress."

Jared's eyes roamed once more over her. "The dress is a keeper and as for our location, I wanted someplace where we could talk and be ourselves and not worry about prying ears."

"Thank you."

The owner came over with a bottle of red wine and poured them both glasses.

"A toast," Jared said. "To learning more about you."

"I can hardly wait." And Morgan couldn't. Something told her the evening was going to be very intriguing. She tapped her glass against his.

* * *

Jared watched Morgan over the rim of his wineglass. Tonight, her dark tresses were in a chic updo showing off her beautiful caramel-brown complexion, which was enhanced by dramatic smoky eye makeup and a nude lip. When she'd opened her hotel door earlier and he'd caught a glimpse of her cleavage, Jared had wanted to push her backward into the room and kiss and stroke her until they both forgot their names.

Instead, they were at his favorite restaurant pretending to act as if the chemistry between them wasn't burning red-hot. His eyes dipped down to her mouth as she spoke about growing up in Las Vegas. He liked the way she licked her lips every so often and his desire stirred. He was drawn to her. He had been from that first night when she stood across from him and he'd seen her warring with herself about confronting her father.

He wondered where her mother was in all this. "So, I know your father is Henry Stewart, but where's your mother? Is she here in Austin or Vegas?"

Morgan shook her head. "She passed away."

"I'm sorry for your loss. You must miss her."

"We weren't close," she continued. "She wasn't there for me growing up."

"Which is why you want your father in your life?"

"You can't miss something you've never had, right?" She reached for her wineglass.

Jared sensed Morgan was covering up her true feelings. She wouldn't be in Austin trying to connect with Henry if she didn't miss having a father. Because without her mother, she was alone. But he wouldn't pry. "My mother is the exact opposite. Mary Robinson is a homemaker and proud of it. Raising me and my brother was her great achievement."

"That's wonderful."

Morgan lowered her lashes and Jared could see the mood taking a downward spiral, so he pivoted. "Tell me about your first boyfriend."

"Great segue there." Morgan chuckled. "I never really had one unless you count Victor Nelson. He wasn't much to speak of. He was a nerd who loved movies. He used to try to sneak kisses in between study hall."

"Sounds mischievous. Did you ever sneak out of the house to go to a club with a fake ID?"

Morgan shook her head. "No, I was pretty tame because I was determined to have a better future than my mama. But something tells me you were the life of the party."

Jared shrugged. "What can I say? I like to have fun, but back then I had a wingman."

"Dane?"

He nodded. "He and I were hell-raisers. Skipping class, making out with girls, driving fast cars. Our parents were at their wits' end until they sent me away to boarding school."

"But that didn't stop you?"

"No." He pursed his lips. "I was just farther out of reach to my parents."

"C'mon, Jared, a guy as good-looking as you had to have been in love once, right?"

Jared looked across the table at Morgan. He hoped she wasn't getting some notion in her head about marriage, babies and white picket fences. Theirs was a mutually beneficial arrangement with an expiration date.

"Never much cared for the notion. How about you? You have some great love that got away?"

Morgan shook her head. "No, can't say that I have."

"Then we're well matched." His eyes traveled to her cleavage. "Though I have to admit I have been in lust." He leaned across the table and placed his hand over hers. Sparks shot through his body and Jared had to work overtime to conceal the explosive desire he felt.

"L-lust."

"Yes," Jared murmured. "Tell me you feel it too."

"I feel like we should order," Morgan stated, cutting him down to size. He did as she asked and motioned the waiter over. The service was spot on and it didn't take long for their meals to arrive and for them to tuck in. As they ate, Jared pondered Morgan's reticence. He didn't understand why was she acting as if she didn't want him when he knew it was far from the truth? The kisses they'd shared thus far were electric. He still remembered the sweet erotic taste of her kiss and his body yearned for more. He would have to remind her how good it was.

Jared's dark intense eyes blazed into Morgan and she had trouble breathing. Her heart was already pounding in her chest and her pulse raced.

Heat. Desire. Want. All those emotions flared through Morgan. She could feel her nipples harden in her dress as she fought the sexual tension swelling between her and Jared. She didn't know what do with it. She was out of her element and didn't have liquor to hide behind.

"Is it wrong to want to explore the passion between us?" Jared inquired. "Because that night in your hotel room—you were prepared to go to bed with me."

Morgan swallowed the lump in her throat. "That was different."

"Please don't tell me you're going to use the cliché excuse you were drinking too much?"

"No, I wasn't going to do that, but I will admit I was emotional that night." Morgan couldn't help missing Jared eyeing her suspiciously as if he knew she was selling a load of hogwash. "Overwhelmed even, by Henry's rejection."

"Perhaps I wouldn't be confused if you weren't hot one minute and cold the next."

"I'm sorry if I'm giving you mixed signals," Morgan said. "So let me be clear. Although I might be your pretend girlfriend that doesn't mean it comes with fringe benefits. Perhaps it's best if we keep our arrangement strictly platonic so as to not complicate our relationship. Now, if you'll excuse me, I'm going to go powder my nose." She bolted upright and ran straight for the ladies' room.

Morgan knew she was running, running from an attraction that frightened her in its intensity. If she allowed herself, he could easily become her first lover.

And would that be so bad? her inner voice asked.

Perhaps it was time for her to stop living in fear and take a risk. If not for love, then for an undeniable passion.

Glancing in the bathroom mirror, Morgan saw her cheeks were flushed and there was a light bead of sweat on her forehead. That's what Jared did to her. He had her all hot and bothered.

Pull it together.

When she returned to their table, Jared was contemplative. "I'm sorry if I've offended you with my directness about intimacy. I will honor your wishes." He glanced behind her. "Ah, dessert is coming. Martin's crème brûlée is to die for."

Morgan gave him a half smile. Had she ruined the night with her past fears and insecurities? Because a guy like Jared wouldn't keep coming back if she kept brushing him off.

Jared backed off. Morgan was spooked and he didn't know why. The attraction between them was undeniable, palpable and inevitable, yet Morgan refused to acknowledge it.

Something was holding her back.

He doubted they'd scratched the surface on her past, but it made him curious to know more. Usually if a woman rebuffed his advances he was on to the next, but Morgan was different and it wasn't because she'd agreed to his arrangement.

It was more. *She* was more. Jared couldn't put his finger on it, but Morgan was intriguing. He would have to arrange their next date quickly in order not to lose momentum and to delve into what made Morgan Stewart tick.

He would have to approach her like a newborn foal. He would have to be delicate and tender. Listen to what she was and wasn't saying. Only then would he stand a chance of figuring out this incredibly complex woman.

After dessert, Jared drove Morgan home. A thick uncomfortable silence hung in the air. Morgan felt as if she'd ruined the evening by being such a prude. A handsome sexy man like Jared Robinson *wanted* her and wasn't afraid to show it. But instead, she'd pushed him away.

No wonder he was angry. Morgan wouldn't be surprised if he decided to end their arrangement altogether. No one wanted a stick-in-the-mud. *Why couldn't she be normal?*

When the car stopped, Morgan realized they'd pulled into the hotel driveway. A valet came to greet them, but Jared shook his head, so they sat with the car idling. Morgan was grateful when Jared spoke first.

"I'm sorry for coming on too strong. You want a purely platonic relationship for the duration of this arrangement, so I will keep my hands to myself." He turned to Morgan and held them up in mock surrender. "But I can't promise you I won't be tempted because you're a beautiful woman."

Morgan hazarded a glance in his direction. "Thank you."

"I took the liberty of paying your hotel bill," Jared continued. "I hope you don't mind. We didn't discuss how this was going to work. Since you're staying in Austin indefinitely, I figured you could stay in one of the apartments in the city we keep for executives. You might be more comfortable there."

"Jared, that sounds wonderful."

"Good. I'll have my assistant arrange everything and call you with the details." He hopped out of the car. Morgan wished they had more time, but instead he was holding her car door open and helping her out of the vehicle.

"We should hang out again before meeting my grandmother," Jared said, walking Morgan inside the hotel to the elevator bank. "Something more comfortable and less like a date."

The ding of the elevator made Morgan involuntarily step toward the doors.

"So what do you say?" Jared asked with a smirk.

"Sounds great. You really do know how to make a comeback."

Jared shrugged. "You ain't seen nothing yet." And with a wink, the door of the elevator closed.

Morgan leaned back against the panels and released a deep sigh. She hadn't messed it up. Jared was still willing to work with her and help her achieve her goals. *So why did it feel as if she'd lost out on something monumental?*

Eight

"So when am I going to meet your girlfriend?" his grandmother asked when she unexpectedly came over for Sunday brunch at Jared's parents' house.

Since it was such a nice day, they were seated out on the lanai. "Soon, Grandmother. We've only known each other a short time and I don't want to frighten her away by taking her to meet the parents so soon."

His grandmother squashed the notion. "Nonsense. That's exactly why she should meet us to be sure she can keep up. We're not an easy bunch to love."

Jared knew that to be true. His grandmother, like his father, believed in the motto of tough love. There was no coddling or hugs in Jared's world. There was only winning and losing. He remembered a time when he was seven years old and had been on the soccer team. Their team had lost the tournament, but they'd each received participation trophies. When he'd gotten home, his father had taken his from Jared.

Better you learn now, son, in life there's one winner. And you lost. Accept it and fight harder to win next time. Jared had never forgotten that lesson.

"I'll bring Morgan over next weekend," Jared finally said.

"Excellent," his grandmother replied. "Let's hope you didn't pick this one up at a strip bar like your brother."

"Ruth, must you be so harsh?" his mother said. "I know you don't approve of Chris's actions, but we don't know the full story."

"I know enough. Chris turned his back on the company, on the family. What more is there to say?"

His mother glanced at his father. True to form, his father never stood up to his own mother, so Jared spoke. "Mom is right. We won't let you speak ill of Chris when he isn't here to defend himself."

His grandmother leaned back in her chair and regarded him. "So you're finally getting a backbone." She sipped her mimosa. "I like it, Jared."

Jared rolled his eyes upward and prayed for patience. How was he supposed to bring Morgan into this dysfunctional family when he could hardly stand it himself? He prayed the tough, fearless Morgan who'd stood up to Henry in front of a crowd of wedding guests was the one who came to dinner on Sunday. Otherwise, his grandmother would eat her for breakfast.

Morgan moved into the stunning corner unit located on the thirty-first floor of Residences at W Austin that afternoon.

Morgan was in awe as she walked through the condominium. The open plan apartment had white oak wood floors, a gourmet kitchen with quartz counters, ten-foot ceilings and floor-to-ceiling windows. The master suite held a large king-size bed and an impressive master bath with double vanity, walk-in shower and garden tub. The California closet would easily fit Morgan's meager clothing.

Morgan plopped herself on the buttery-soft leather couch and sighed. Was this the lifestyle she would have grown accustomed to if she'd been raised a Stewart? It was certainly something she could get used to, but she mustn't let herself. She was arm candy for Jared for a limited period, but that didn't stop her from having growing feelings for him.

Morgan found him charming, funny and sexy as hell. There was more to Jared than the playboy he portrayed. She wondered if he would show her more or continue to hide behind the facade. She hoped to find out on their next date. Morgan was excited at the prospect. Being with Jared connected her to the sensual side of her nature, but it also put all her senses on alert.

Troy's assault had made Morgan fear intimacy. But surely, a skilled man such as Jared could help her overcome those fears, couldn't he? *Could she allow more to transpire?* Morgan wasn't sure because losing control frightened her more than anything. On the other hand, when she was in Jared's arms, the world melted away and she felt completely alive.

Was he worth the risk?

Jared wanted to strangle the high-end client he'd been dealing with on Wednesday. As CEO, he didn't usually handle the sales side of Robinson Holdings, but apparently Chris already had this in the works. So Jared was playing real estate agent to an entitled multimillionaire, chauffeuring him around town when he had better ways to occupy his time. A certain dark-haired beauty came to mind.

While the client took another walk through the estate Jared was showing him, Jared stepped away to check in on his pseudo girlfriend.

"I'm surprised to hear from you in the middle of the day," Morgan commented when she picked up.

"Is that how you respond to your boyfriend?"

She chuckled on the other end of the line. "I'm sorry." She cleared her throat. "Let me try again." She paused for a beat. "Hi, honey, how's your day going?"

Jared smiled inwardly. "That's better. What are you up to?"

"Researching some positions I'm interested in in Los Angeles."

Jared's stomach sank. Why was the thought of Morgan going back home so distasteful? Was it because he was enjoying having her around? "Good for you. You'll let me know if there's anything I can do?"

"Of course. But I'm sure that's not why you called."

He laughed. "No, I was calling about this weekend. I thought we could get together on Saturday. I have someplace I'd like to take you. We'll need to get started a bit early in the afternoon if that's okay?"

"Should I wear anything special?"

"No need. It's our chill date, remember?"

"That's right. I can hardly wait to see you dressed down and looking like an everyday Joe."

"I doubt that's possible," Jared responded, "though

you should consider enhancing your wardrobe while we're together. I'll have my assistant set up some accounts at the fashionable boutiques."

"Jared…that's not necessary. I'm not a charity case. I can dress myself."

"I know, but you're with me now and you'll be expected to be dressed in the latest designer clothing."

"Fine."

She was too quick to acquiesce to his request, but Jared let it go because his client was walking straight toward him. "I gotta go, but I'll see you on Saturday."

When Saturday arrived, Jared was happy. His date with Morgan was today. The rest of the workweek had gone by quickly. He'd sat through endless meetings about their next project in Lady Bird Lake and dealt with the board's reticence about his position as interim CEO. Jared was doing his best to show he was capable, but he wasn't used to the early mornings and long days.

Pulling into the Residences at the W, he saw Morgan waiting for him outside. She sashayed toward the door of his Porsche Cayman GTS and jumped in wearing inky-dark skinny jeans that hugged her curves and a ruffled one-shoulder top that raised the flirt factor.

She gave him a warm smile and Jared felt his heart kick in his chest. "Hey."

"Hey." She leaned over and to his surprise, brushed her lips across his.

"What was that for?" he asked when she lifted her head.

"I'm playing my role in case anyone—" she inclined her head toward the valets "—was looking."

She was right, but he wished she'd kissed him because she wanted to—because she missed him as he'd missed her all week—instead of out of necessity. "Of course."

"So where are you taking me?" Morgan asked, buckling her seat belt.

He gave her a quick glance as he pulled away from the curb. "You'll see."

As they drove, Morgan told him about her experience shopping in Austin's high-end boutiques. "I can't believe you didn't give me a limit. I have never spent so much money on clothes in my entire life."

Jared glanced at her in consternation. "My assistant told me you didn't spend that much. I was expecting a larger amount."

"I'm not spending all your money, Jared. Otherwise, I'd feel too much like my mother. She took money from her boyfriends all the time. I understand I have to dress the part, so I bought enough to get me by."

Jared sensed that the resentment Morgan had toward her deceased mother went deep and felt it best to let it rest. "All right, but if you ever need more, say the word."

Morgan glanced at him. "I appreciate that." He watched as her eyes traveled the length of him and back up to meet his gaze. "Jeans and a T-shirt look good on you."

"Why, thank you." Jared grinned from ear to ear.

Their conversation was light. Jared regaled her with stories about his week at the office. Eventually they drove through the gates of Avalon Memory Care. Morgan immediately turned to him. "What is this place?"

"It's a center to help those affected by Alzheimer's, dementia and other cognitive issues."

Her brow furrowed. "I don't understand."

Jared pulled his Porsche into a parking space and turned to face her. "My grandfather is here. He suffers from Alzheimer's. At first, the progression was slow. Sometimes he wouldn't remember me and Chris and would think we were our father. So he had a nurse at their home, but then it became worse. My grandmother couldn't—correction, *wouldn't*—deal with it, so she put him here." Jared didn't wait for more questions. Instead he bounded out of the door and Morgan did the same.

As he came toward her, Morgan touched his arm. "It has to be hard watching someone you love slip away bit by bit." Her voice caught. "I'm terribly sorry."

"It is, but let's hope today is a good day." Jared reached for her hand and Morgan allowed him to entwine their fingers together as they walked toward the entrance.

Sylvia, one of the many nurses on staff, greeted him. "Jared, it's so good to see you. Who'd you bring with you?"

"Sylvia, I'd like you to meet my girlfriend, Morgan."

Sylvia clasped Morgan's free hand in hers. "Great to meet you, honey." She turned to Jared. "I'm so happy you keep coming, Jared. I know it gets harder each time."

Jared swallowed the lump in his throat. "I can't leave him here and forget about him. He's my grandpa."

Sylvia smiled. "You're a good man. Follow me." She led them down the hall, which although clean smelled like disinfectant. When they reached his grandfather's room, Sylvia knocked and then opened the door.

Jared went to walk inside, and Morgan squeezed his hand firmly. "I'm all right," he said.

His grandfather sat in a rocker watching television. He wore trousers and his favorite blue-and-white-checkered button-down shirt and loafers. When he glanced up and recognition crossed his face, Jared exhaled audibly.

"Anthony, look who's hear to see you!" Sylvia said.

"Jared! Come here ole boy." His grandfather opened his arms and Jared released Morgan's hand to rush into them. He squeezed his grandfather in a warm embrace.

"I'll leave you to your visit." Sylvia waved and left them alone.

His grandfather grasped both sides of Jared's face. "Let me have a look at you." He gave him the once-over. "You're a handsome young man and staying fit. It's how I kept Ruth interested in me."

"Grandpa." Jared went to Morgan, who stood immobilized near the door. "I'd like you to meet my girl-friend, Morgan."

She moved toward him and his grandfather wrapped her up in a big hug just like he used to do when he and Chris were little. Jared missed those days.

His grandfather kept his arm around Morgan and turned to Jared. "She's a real looker. I'm not surprised you fell. Bet you fell hard too."

Jared stared at Morgan. *Is that what happened?* No, Jared dismissed the notion. He was attracted to Morgan. It was nothing more than that.

"So tell me…" his grandfather said, sitting down in his rocker. "How did you and my grandson meet?"

"We met at a wedding," Morgan answered. "I made a big fool of myself and Jared rescued me."

His grandfather gave him a conspiratorial wink. "Is that right? I dare say it was because of your over-whelming beauty."

"That too," Jared responded with a smirk. And even Morgan laughed.

"I'm glad you were able to break through the bar-rier. Morgan, was it?"

"Yes, sir."

"Ever since he was a little kid, Jared's always been the guarded one. My other grandson, Chris—well, he's an open book, but Jared, you could never tell what he was feeling. He always kind of played it close to the vest. So I'm happy to see you're getting underneath those layers."

When Morgan looked at Jared, it felt as if she was peering into his very soul, so he looked away. *She* un-nerved him because his grandfather was right—Jared never showed his hand because growing up his feel-ings had never mattered. Yet when he was with Mor-gan, Jared *felt* everything.

Was this how the other half lived? Because if so, Jared wanted no part of it. He would stay in his unfeel-ing world because it was safe there and didn't require him to be vulnerable.

Morgan was stunned Jared had brought her to meet his grandfather. He'd allowed her to see a different side she'd suspected existed, but he rarely showed. Jared wasn't some cookie-cutter playboy. He cared and was fiercely loyal to his family. During their visit to the fa-cility, she'd learned that Jared came to see his grand-father often. He didn't merely pay lip service and come a handful of times a year like on birthdays or holidays.

After they had lunch on the terrace where several other families gathered with their loved ones, Morgan watched Jared and his grandfather play checkers. She noticed he could have easily won, but he allowed his grandfather to beat him because he didn't remember all the moves.

Morgan smiled as she watched the two men. Anthony Robinson was an older version of Jared with warm dark brown eyes, tawny skin and straight white teeth. But it was the mannerisms, the way they both cocked their head to one side or pondered their next move that made her see the real similarities.

Eventually, the senior Robinson tired and they walked him back to his room.

"Morgan," Anthony said when he finally sat back down in his rocker. "You take care of my boy."

"I will." She smiled because she intended to keep that promise. She leaned over and gave his hand a squeeze. Stepping away, she watched Jared with his grandfather.

When he looked her way, Morgan could have sworn there were tears in Jared's eyes, but he quickly recovered his composure. "You ready to go?"

"I am." She slid her hand inside Jared's as they walked to the car.

Jared's mood was somber as he pulled away. "Are you okay?"

"Hmmm…" He sounded distracted. "Yes, I'm fine."

"It's okay if you do want to talk."

"About my grandpa?" Jared asked. "What could I say? I hate having him there with strangers? Or maybe that I wish our family would take care of him? Is that what you're looking for?"

Morgan didn't take the bait. She knew Jared's underlying anger wasn't directed at her. "I understand it's hard seeing him there, but at least he has you."

Jared snorted. "He would be better off with Chris."

"Stop it!" Her raised voice caught his attention and he stared at her in shock. "Stop putting yourself down, Jared. You're the one who visits him regularly. You're the one who's busting your butt working night and day to cover for Chris because he chose to leave without letting anyone know. So I won't accept you demeaning yourself and saying your contribution to your family isn't as important."

The car came to a sudden stop and Morgan turned to him. Their eyes met and held, and that was all it took for him to lean forward and crush his mouth to hers. Morgan closed her eyes and embraced the kiss. It was gentle at first, but Jared quickly deepened it, sliding his hand through her hair as his tongue caressed hers. Morgan clung to him, returning his passion until he slowly released her.

She blinked up at him, dazed.

"No one has ever defended me like that," Jared said, his voice hoarse with lust. "I'm sorry for coming on so strong again. I promised I wasn't going to get handsy. Yet every time I'm around you, I can't seem to control myself."

"I can't explain what comes over me either," Morgan said honestly.

"What are we going to do about it?"

"I thought we agreed to remain platonic."

"It seems neither one of us is keeping that promise very well, but since we're back at square one, we should get a move on it to part two of the day." Moving back to his seat, Jared put the car in gear and drove them to the garage of a downtown high-rise.

"Is our date over?" Morgan inquired.

Jared chuckled. "No. We're having dinner at my place." He exited the vehicle and opened her door. There were several sports cars parked alongside Jared's Porsche including a Ferrari.

"Let me guess." She inclined her head. "These are yours?"

He grinned unabashedly. "What can I say, I like fast cars. C'mon, I'll take you upstairs."

The elevator zoomed to the fiftieth floor, taking them straight to Jared's penthouse. The dark color palette was rich and masculine with cool neutral undertones that suited him. Unlike her apartment, the floors were a dark ebony hardwood and the kitchen had European-style cabinets with dark gray quartz countertops and a black hexagon backsplash. The penthouse had breathtaking views. Austin could be seen from every room and the balcony, which had a plunge pool and spa.

"This place is very you," Morgan said, looking out at the city. She turned and leaned against the railing. "I can see you bringing ladies up here to wow them with the view before you…" Her voice trailed off when Jared came to the balcony entrance and stood watching her.

Jared finished her sentence. "Before I take them to bed? I'm sorry to disappoint you, Morgan, but I don't bring women home. It's my retreat from the world. A safe haven if you will."

"So…"

"You're the only woman I've brought here," he replied. "Would you like a drink?"

"I'd love one." Morgan swallowed the lump in her

throat. *She* was the only woman he'd brought here. *Did it mean he might like her more than he cared to admit?*

Minutes later, Jared returned carrying two glasses of a dark brown liquid. "Cheers!" He tapped his glass against hers.

She swallowed, if for nothing else than to ease the ache in her nether regions from the dark look in Jared's eyes. The alcohol burned going down but she welcomed it. "So what's for dinner?"

Jared chuckled. "Oh I'm no cook, but I'm excellent at ordering. Our dinner should be arriving any moment."

"Arriving?"

"A personal chef is delivering the food. I hope you don't mind."

Morgan drank more of her drink. "Not at all. But I could have cooked for us."

"Really?"

"Yes, I'm a pretty good cook. I had to learn how to at a young age. If I didn't, I would've been eating cereal and peanut butter and jelly sandwiches every day. My mother never remembered to shop so I had to fend for myself."

"Sounds like it was tough on you growing up."

"It was. I yearned for my father to come one day and take me away from it all. It was a silly wish." Morgan finished off the rest of her drink.

"Not silly," Jared replied. The doorbell rang and he glanced at the open doorway. "That would be our dinner."

Morgan followed him inside and watched as the chef removed the meals he'd brought. There were starters, entrées, even dessert; one for each of them. Once he'd gone, she and Jared helped themselves, piling chopped strawberry pecan salad and chicken piccata with capers on their plates.

"Looks delicious," Morgan said once they were seated at an enormous dining room table that could seat upward of eight.

"Yes, it does," Jared replied and somehow Morgan knew he wasn't talking about the food.

As they ate their meal, Jared tried his best not to think about their explosive kiss in the car. He'd intended to honor his word and keep their arrangement platonic, but Morgan had spoken up for him passionately. More than any person ever had.

This beautiful, feisty brunette was turning him inside out. He didn't quite recognize himself. The night they'd met, he'd been a gentleman, a protector ensuring no other man took advantage of her. Even when she'd brought him up to her room, he found himself taking care of her when she became ill.

And today, he'd wanted her to see a different side of him. To truly *know* him. She was special and he'd wanted his grandpa to meet her. And doggone it, if his grandpa hadn't hit the nail on the head when he'd commented on Morgan breaking through his reserve.

"Is there anything I should know to prepare for dinner with your grandmother tomorrow? Any deep dark family secrets?"

"Nothing so melodramatic," Jared replied. "My grandmother can smell a rat. So just be yourself. Honest. Direct. And she'll love you."

"I hope so. Our whole arrangement depends on my convincing her."

Jared eyed her. "Despite that, if you needed my help until you figured out your next step, I'd help you."

She stared at him in disbelief. "Why would you do that?"

"I like you, Morgan." Jared smiled. "A lot." He couldn't believe how forthcoming he was being.

"The feeling's mutual."

Her honesty was a breath of fresh air. There were no games or tricks. What you saw was what you got. And if he had his way, they'd get to know each other a whole lot better before their arrangement was over.

Nine

"Stop fidgeting," Jared said when he and Morgan stood outside the door of his grandmother's estate the following evening.

"I'm not."

"Yes, you are." He grabbed her hand and Morgan felt the frisson of electricity go up her arm as it always did when Jared was near. Tonight was no different. He not only looked impeccably gorgeous, but he smelled divine, like citrus and spice.

He rang the doorbell and a uniformed butler greeted them. "Antoine, this is my girl, Morgan. Morgan, meet Antoine. He's been with my grandmother for years."

"Lovely to meet you." Morgan offered her hand and Antoine brought it to his lips.

"A pleasure, madam. Allow me to show you the way."

"You know I don't stand on ceremony, Antoine, even with my girlfriend here. Where's grandmother?"

"In the living room."

"C'mon," Jared said. "It's time to meet the queen."

Morgan walked on leaden feet down the marble corridor. She knew it was nothing for Jared to be around such opulence, but this home put Henry's estate to shame. Morgan could feel the history.

Jared led her to a room where a slender woman about five-foot-eight was sitting. Her blondish gray hair was in a sophisticated bob and she wore a killer designer sheath.

"Jared, you finally arrived. I was beginning to worry," she said, then her glance flickered to Morgan at his side. "And you must be Jared's girlfriend?"

"Grandmother, this is Morgan Stewart. Morgan, this is my grandmother, Ruth Robinson."

His grandmother's brow furrowed. "Stewart, did you say? Come over so I can have a look at you."

Jared released her hand and Morgan pasted a smile onto her face and moved closer. "Mrs. Robinson, it's a pleasure to meet you."

"And you, my dear, are definitely one of Henry's offspring. You have his trademark hazel eyes and his coloring. But why is this the first I'm hearing about you? If I recall, Henry only has one daughter. Fallon, I believe her name is."

"Grandmother, you're being indelicate," Jared admonished.

"I'm merely speaking the truth." She glanced at Morgan. She could tell the woman missed nothing. It was why Morgan had splurged and gone to the salon to have her hair and makeup expertly done. She couldn't afford any mistakes. "You can appreciate that, can't you, dear?"

"Honesty is always the best policy," Morgan stated with a tight smile. "And to answer your question, yes, Henry Stewart is my father, but you might want to remind him of that fact."

"Is he being difficult?" Ruth inquired.

"He downright refuses to acknowledge my existence," Morgan responded. "But that didn't stop me from taking Stewart as my rightful legal name."

Ruth smiled. "Good for you. I like a woman with chutzpah." She turned to Jared. "However did you find Morgan? She's not one of the usual bimbos you traipse about town with."

Morgan noticed Jared's jaw clench and she sensed he wanted to rebut, but he said, "Morgan and I met through Dane."

"Ah, the young man who used to be a troublemaker. I'm glad to see he's married and settled down with a family. Dare I hope you could do the same?"

"Don't push your luck," Jared responded.

"I beg to differ. Morgan is a breath of fresh air and I'm going to claim her," Ruth said, eyeing Morgan. "Come." She patted the seat beside her. "Sit beside me. Jared, be a dear and fix us a drink while we get to know one another."

They chatted about inconsequential topics until dinner. Jared was the consummate date. He drew Morgan's chair out and waited for her to sit down before lowering his tall frame into the seat across from her. She supposed he sat there on purpose so he could focus his full attention on her.

Over the next couple of hours, Ruth was direct, gently quizzing Morgan on her background—where she came from, where she went to school and where she worked. And just as Jared told her to do, Morgan was honest.

But nothing could stop the intangible spark of sexual attraction shooting back and forth across the table or the predatory hunger in Jared's gaze. Morgan wondered if he looked at every woman that way. *Did he make them all feel as if they were the most beautiful woman in the world?* His simple gesture of asking if she'd like more wine made Morgan feel the sizzle. Her eyes darted to his grandmother but she was none the wiser.

"I come from humble beginnings, Mrs. Robinson," Morgan said once they'd retired to the sitting room for coffee. Jared opted for something much stronger. "But I've prided myself in always being able to support myself."

Jared had been quiet for most of the night, content to let the two women dominate much of the conversation. Occasionally he put in an anecdote here or there. But all the while, he'd openly stared at her when he thought she wasn't looking.

An involuntary tremble went through Morgan at his searing gaze. What would it be like if she allowed herself to do more? If she ran her hands down his back, touched the corded muscles of his arms, felt the warmth of his skin? If she laced her fingers around his head and pulled him down to taste the sweetness of his mouth?

"Morgan?"

She blinked rapidly. Oh God, she'd been caught daydreaming. Morgan turned her gaze to Ruth and forced her expression not to betray where her thoughts had strayed.

"You were stating how you supported yourself," Ruth offered.

"Oh yes, I put myself through college, working two, sometimes three jobs to cover the books and expenses my scholarship didn't."

"See, Jared." His grandmother pointed to him. "This is what it's like when you've earned what you have."

"Thank you, ma'am." She'd rather enjoyed having someone older to talk to.

"You've impressed me, Morgan, and that's not easy to do."

"Believe her," Jared said. "I've stopped trying."

"No, you haven't," Morgan replied. "Right now, you've been working day and night at Robinson Holdings to show your grandmother and the board you're no slacker."

Ruth clapped her hands in glee. "Bravo, dear girl. You not only silenced him, but had my grandson's back." She looked at Jared. "You must do all you can to keep her."

The possessive look Jared bestowed on her caused a hard shiver to rock Morgan's body. "Oh, I intend to." He glanced down at his Rolex. "In the meantime, it's late. I should be getting Morgan home."

His grandmother rose to her feet and gave Morgan a spontaneous hug. Morgan glanced at Jared and his eyes were wide with surprise. "I'm happy you came this evening," Ruth said. "My family and I are going to our compound next weekend. We usually go boating and ride horses, skeet shoot and picnic. It's rather bourgeois, but I would love for you to join us."

Morgan didn't have to worry because Jared answered. "Of course. We'll be there."

A broad smile spread across Ruth's lips. "I look forward to it."

As they walked to the car, Morgan felt like the evening was a resounding success. She'd convinced Ruth she was Jared's legitimate girlfriend, and she suspected the older woman had taken a liking to her. So why as he helped her into the Porsche did Morgan feel like she'd done something wrong?

Jared reflected on the night as he settled into the driver's seat. He couldn't put his finger on what made Morgan different from any of the other women he'd dated, only that she had charmed his grandmother of all people. Ruth had a genuine affection for Morgan and her ability to battle against the odds and come out on the other side. And she'd given Morgan a *hug*. She didn't even hug Jared.

"Jared?" Morgan touched his arm. "What's wrong?"

"Nothing."

"Tonight went great, don't you think?"

He sighed and hazarded a glance at her. Morgan had looked incredible tonight. Her makeup was flawless and she was more beautiful than ever. Her cheekbones were defined, her eyes smoky and sensual and that wide, pretty mouth of hers had captured his attention all night. White-hot desire gripped him when he allowed his gaze to linger on the soft mounds displayed in the low-cut neckline of the simple black jersey dress she wore. He'd tried hard not focus all evening on her décolletage.

"You're a charmer," Jared finally answered. "You won my grandmother over."

"That's good, right?"

"Yes, it is."

"Then why do I think I've failed you in some way?" she asked, her face twisted in consternation.

"You haven't, Morgan." Jared started the engine to effectively end the conversation. He would drive her home and go back to his place and take a long hot shower. The problem was, he didn't know how long he could keep dating Morgan and not ease the permanent sexual ache he had whenever they were together. *How was he going to survive a weekend at his family's compound?*

When they pulled into the W, Jared left the car idling and came around to Morgan's door. He helped her out, but when he made no move to go in, she looked at him expectantly.

"It's best we say good-night here," Jared said. He couldn't go up to her apartment, not when all he wanted to do was strip the dress from her body and sink deep inside her. He moved toward her and rubbed her arms, which felt chilled, then leaned forward placing his forehead against hers. "Thank you. I appreciate everything you did tonight."

"You do?" She sounded as if she was surprised.

"Absolutely, but you should go inside now so I can do the honorable thing."

"What if I don't want you to be honorable?"

"Morgan…" he murmured, but his resolve was gone, especially when she went on tippy toe to sweep her mouth over his, tantalizing him with a promise of sweeter delight. Jared cupped her neck and drew her to him. This time, he kissed her and when he felt a tremor run through her, he didn't stop. He continued moving his lips over hers, seeking, tasting and enticing. When she parted her lips, his tongue slipped inside and tangled with hers in an urgent frenzy.

It was only the sound of the valet clearing his throat that reminded Jared they were outside the hotel in a public place. "I have to go, Morgan. We'll talk soon."

With effort, considering the tightness of his groin, Jared made it back inside the car and pulled away. In his rearview, he saw Morgan still standing there, touching her lips.

Ten

The last couple of days since the dinner with Jared and his grandmother had been marvelous. Was it because their relationship had taken a turn? Morgan had not only convinced Ruth of their blossoming romance, but Jared had taken her to meet his grandfather.

Yesterday, she'd surprised Jared at his office and whisked him away for lunch. Sure, it was a sandwich in the park, but it was something a girlfriend, someone who cared for him, would do. And Morgan cared. She was trying hard not to get carried away by this fake relationship, but she couldn't act as if she hadn't developed feelings for him.

The deeper they got into this arrangement, the harder it was to pull back. There was a palpable sexual attraction between them that could no longer be ignored, though they were giving their best impression it didn't exist.

Morgan was thankful when Fallon and Ayden invited her for coffee. Morgan hadn't seen Fallon since the day at the mansion when she'd told Fallon she didn't want anything to do with the Stewarts. It wasn't her finest moment, so Morgan was determined to make an effort.

When she arrived, however, another Stewart was waiting for her. Someone she'd been hoping not to face.

Dane.

She saw his two bodyguards chatting with each other as she went into the deserted coffee shop, where the workers stood mesmerized by her movie star big brother. She was unfazed by his good looks—smooth tapioca coloring, strong jawline, dark brown eyes and bushy eyebrows. Dane wore sunglasses and his usual dark jeans, T-shirt and old leather jacket. But when Morgan entered, he ripped the sunglasses off to glare at her. "You have a lot of explaining to do."

Morgan gulped as she walked toward him. "When did you and Iris get back?"

"Day before yesterday," Dane replied. "And we came back to a firestorm about my illegitimate baby sister. So I left Iris and Jayden and came straight here. What the hell, Morgan? You've been working for me for over a year. Why on God's green earth didn't you tell me we're related?"

"I'll explain, but I don't appreciate being ambushed."

"Fallon was worried you wouldn't show if she told you I was coming."

Morgan folded her arms across her chest. "What

about her and Ayden? Are they coming? Or was this all an elaborate ruse so you can give me the business?"

"Sit down, Morgan," Dane ordered.

Morgan recognized his boss voice and rather than argue took a seat at the round table beside him.

"Of course they're coming, but we, you and me," he pointed between them, "need to clear the air."

Dane was right. She owed him an apology. "I'm sorry."

"Was that so hard?" Dane inquired, his brown eyes narrowing on her.

"No. I was wrong to keep my identity hidden from you."

"So why did you?"

Morgan shrugged. Why was it so hard to face Dane? She'd told this story several times since, but to him, the brother she idolized, she felt like she had cotton in her mouth.

"Morgan?"

She inhaled deeply. "I was afraid to tell you. What if you didn't believe me? Henry doesn't. I thought I'd get to know you first, but the more I did, the more I liked and respected you. How could I not? You accepted Jayden and Iris into your life when you could have lost everything. I was impressed by your valor."

"I'm no hero, Morgan," Dane replied. "I'm a man with flaws like everyone else. Don't go putting me on some pedestal. It's hard to meet folks' expectations from up there."

"That's what I love about you, Dane. You give it to me straight." Morgan covered her mouth. "I didn't mean *love*. I…" Her voice trailed off when she saw the amusement in his eyes.

He reached across the table and placed his rather large hand over hers. "It's okay, Morgan. I've always looked at you as the little sister I never had, so I have no problem accepting you into the family. I just wish you would have gone about this another way."

"I'm sorry for bringing you and Iris back into the spotlight after Jayden's illness," Morgan replied. "I didn't think ahead. I just wanted Henry to claim me as his own."

"My father is a stubborn man," Dane responded. "I'm not sure if he ever will, but I'll support you, kid."

Morgan beamed, and despite herself, happy tears slid down her cheeks. Dane leaned across to wipe them away with his thumbs.

"Oh, Lord," a female voice said from behind them, "please tell me you didn't make her cry, Dane."

Morgan knew that voice and spun around to see Fallon and Ayden at the door.

"Welcome back, bro." Ayden managed to lift Dane off his feet even though he was six feet tall, because Ayden had a few inches on him.

"How was the honeymoon?" Fallon asked, winking at Dane.

"Nothing I care to comment on with my big sis," Dane responded good-naturedly. "Come here." He wrapped his arms around Fallon. "How's Nora?"

"Still furious with Daddy," Fallon replied. "At least she's moved back home, though they are sleeping in separate rooms."

"He deserves it," Dane said. "He cheated on her. Though she shouldn't necessarily be surprised. He did the same to Ayden's mom."

"Don't be heartless, Dane. She should at least expect loyalty from her husband."

"I don't disagree, but this is our father we're talking about."

Morgan was overwhelmed watching their interaction. *These were her siblings.* She shrank back from the three of them. They were already a trio. *Where did she fit in?*

"And where do you think you're going?" Ayden asked. He quickly lifted her off her feet too and into his embrace.

Morgan couldn't resist releasing a big laugh. "Put me down, you big lug." She swatted him on the arm and he set her on her feet.

"It's nice to have the *four* of us together in one place," Fallon said, and her eyes went to Morgan. When her sister smiled, Morgan felt relieved Fallon wasn't holding a grudge.

"Let's have a coffee." Ayden looked around the room and noticed the store was empty. "What's the deal? Where is everybody?"

"My team paid the shop to close for the afternoon," Dane responded.

"Don't you think that's a bit extra?" Fallon replied.

"Nope. They even made everyone sign confidentiality agreements."

"It must suck to be you sometimes," Ayden commented.

"Hey, don't hate on my brother." Morgan didn't realize she'd spoken aloud until three curious sets of eyes landed on her. "I mean…" she attempted to backpedal.

Fallon walked over to Morgan and wrapped her arm

around Morgan's shoulders. "He's your brother too. You can defend him."

Morgan mouthed *Thank you*.

"Well, I'm going to have a frozen coffee concoction," Fallon stated and headed to the counter where an attendant waited silently at the register.

"I'll join you." Ayden stepped away to look at the menu.

"Please tell me you'll join me for a real coffee." Dane looked at Morgan. "Or are you going to have your usual, a café mocha?"

Morgan's brow furrowed. "You know what coffee I like?"

"Why wouldn't I?" Dane asked, peering at her. "You've worked for me for a while now."

"I never thought you paid any attention to me. I was your assistant, after all."

Dane stared at her incredulously. "You've been more than an assistant, Morgan. You helped make my life easier."

Morgan smiled at his heartfelt words. "That means a lot, thank you. And to answer your question, I will have a café mocha. Who drinks regular coffee anyway?"

Morgan shared how well the coffee meeting went later that evening on the phone with Jared. They'd stayed at the coffee shop for hours until Fallon and Ayden both commented they had to get home to their kids. Morgan was excited to have a niece and nephew. Dane was headed back to Los Angeles to Iris and Jayden. Seeing her siblings go home to their respective families made Morgan long to have a family of her own.

"That's wonderful, Morgan," Jared said. "I'm glad to see you bonding with your siblings. I wish I could do the same."

"Is Chris still MIA?"

"Yep. I've left countless messages for him and he hasn't answered a single one of them," Jared responded. "I wish he would just talk to me and tell me what's going on. Maybe I could help. And I could certainly use his advice when it comes to managing Robinson Holdings."

"I imagine it's been a trial by fire."

"You can say that again." Jared chuckled. "But I'll carry on. I don't have much choice. I'm the only Robinson left standing."

"True, but don't you find it rewarding to have your family need you?"

"Yeah, I suppose I do," Jared said. "They've never looked at me as anything other than a screwup, and suddenly I'm their salvation. It's a bit disconcerting. My grandmother is usually calling me about how I've embarrassed the family with my shenanigans, but now she's talking shop and asking my opinion."

"You've always had it in you, Jared," Morgan responded. "Perhaps you needed to be put to the test to realize your true potential."

"When did you become so wise, Morgan Stewart?"

"Maybe because I had to grow up early and take care of myself." Silence ensued on the other end and Morgan realized he'd meant it to be a rhetorical question.

"You're not alone now," Jared murmured softly. "You have your siblings and you have me."

"For a limited time," Morgan reminded him. The

terms of their arrangement were never far from her mind. If she was honest, she would like to date Jared, *for real*, to see where their relationship would go, but he'd made it abundantly clear he was not in it for the long haul.

"Um…" Jared cleared his throat. "Yeah…that's right. So, are you ready for a weekend of fun with the Robinsons?"

"I am. After hearing about your parents, I'm eager to finally meet them."

"Good, I'll pick you up at three on Friday afternoon and we'll get an early jump on traffic. How's that sound?"

"Great, see you then." Morgan stared at her phone after he'd hung up. Was it her imagination or had their conversation ended on a sharp note after she'd brought up the short time they had remaining together? She wished it weren't so, but she had to keep telling herself not to get too attached to Jared before she got hurt.

Morgan inhaled deeply. *Who was she kidding?* She was already falling for the guy.

Jared rose from the sofa he'd been lounging on while talking to Morgan. She sounded so happy about connecting with her siblings. He was happy because he sensed deep down, she wanted to be part of something bigger. And now, as a Stewart, she would have in-laws, nieces and nephews.

He wanted that for her because it wasn't something *he* could give her. He could tell Morgan was growing attached to him. They were spending an awful lot of time together. He too was starting to feel a connection he'd never felt. Jared could talk to her about anything—

work, family, it didn't matter—because Morgan offered good advice and positivity, something sorely missing in his life. She championed him and it was a heady feeling.

But it made Jared wary. He couldn't be her hero. He wasn't built that way. He was the lothario who knew how to show a woman a good time and please her in the bedroom. But offer more? He wasn't capable of it. Or at least he didn't think he was. He'd never stayed in a relationship long enough to find out.

Having been blessed with good looks, he been pursued by the opposite sex since he was a teenager. He'd relished the attention of the nubile women who'd flocked to him. Many had tried and been unsuccessful in their attempts to get Jared to want more during the affairs, until Morgan. *Was it because none of them could hold a candle up to her?*

She was the most innocent and guileless of the women he'd dated. Jared didn't want to hurt Morgan, yet he couldn't deny he wanted to make love to her. Whenever they were together, Jared felt not only his heart contract and expand, but his trousers get tighter. He was doing his best to keep his distance, but he suspected two days in the country was sure to either drive him crazy or Morgan into his bed. And if it was the latter, Jared wouldn't mind it one bit.

Eleven

"Your family calls this a compound?" Morgan asked that Friday afternoon. Jared had driven them about thirty minutes outside the city toward Lake Austin and had slid past two private wrought iron gates. The Porsche Cayman GTS was now on a tree-lined street with hundreds of massive oaks.

"My grandpa bought this place because of the view, but he also wanted to be surrounded by nature," Jared replied. "There's a lot of white-tailed deer, spring-fed creeks and limestone and granite outcroppings. When we were kids, he used to take Chris and me out kayaking and fishing. But if that's not your speed there's some local wineries, boutique shopping and chef-owned restaurants. So there's plenty to do."

Morgan absorbed Jared's words and thought about the weekend ahead. She wasn't afraid of meeting Jared's parents or spending time with his grandmother again. She liked Ruth. She was worried, however, about the sleeping arrangements. Morgan was certain everyone assumed they'd want one room and it wasn't like she could request a separate one. It would raise a red flag. So, she was going to have sleep beside Jared for the next two nights. Given how red-hot their kisses had been, Morgan was afraid of what might happen.

Jared drove past a long white perimeter fence with horses grazing in the field and Morgan had to ask, "You have horses? How many acres is this place?"

Jared shrugged. "I don't know. A couple hundred." The car curved around a winding paved driveway and stopped in front of a two-story brick-and-stone veneer mansion with medieval castle-style doors. Across from the house, there was an exceptionally large coy pond.

Morgan didn't wait for Jared to help her as she opened her door and got out, staring openmouthed at their beautifully serene surroundings.

"Want a tour?" Jared asked.

Morgan beamed with pleasure. "I'd love one."

Jared grabbed her hand and said, "We'll start outdoors."

The compound had not only the main house, but had smaller homes throughout the estate. It came complete with a theater, its own gym with indoor basketball court, game room, an entertaining pavilion, two pools with spas, a boat storage facility, a baseball field, a volleyball court and a chipping and putting green that overlooked the lake.

"I feel like I'm at a resort," Morgan said after the tour ended at the main house. She helped Jared with the bags and he procured a key and opened the front door.

"Hello!" Jared called out when they entered the foyer with a baby grand piano front and center. When no one answered, he turned to her. "We must be the first arrival."

"No, you're not." Antoine came rushing toward them down the hall. "I'm sorry I wasn't here to greet you. The staff and I are still getting ready for the weekend. We learned your brother, Chris, and his girlfriend are joining us."

"Chris is coming?" Jared's voice rose several octaves.

Antoine nodded. "Was it as much of a surprise to you as it was to your grandmother? Allow me to show you to your quarters."

As she walked up the winding staircase behind Jared, Morgan surveyed her surroundings, noting the vaulted ceilings and elaborate chandeliers. Eventually, Antoine stopped in front of a large oak door and swung it open. The room contained a four poster bed covered in a steel-colored velvet duvet with tons of pillows, including one made of Mongolian fur. A beautiful stone fireplace sat across from the bed, giving the space a cozy atmosphere.

"Your en suite bath is to the right and has towels and toiletries," Antoine said. "Let me know if you need anything else."

"Sure thing." Jared closed the door behind him when he left.

"So." Morgan looked around the room, There were two accent chairs next to a table, but there was nowhere else for them to sleep but the bed.

"I can sleep on the floor," Jared offered, sensing her discomfort, "though I have to admit I'm not looking forward to the prospect. It can get pretty cool along the water at night."

Morgan offered a smile. "I wouldn't do that to you. This is your family's home. Plus, it's just two nights. I'm sure we can share a bed together. It'll be a piece of cake, right?"

Jared's pupils flared. "We should go," he said after several moments. "See who else has arrived."

"Like Chris?"

"Heck yeah. I have a major bone to pick with him."

Morgan was glad for the easy out, but she knew it was only a temporary reprieve. It wouldn't be long before they'd have to share that bed.

Jared was desperate to get out of the bedroom. If he stayed any longer, he wasn't going to be responsible for his actions. Sleeping beside Morgan night after night was going to be agony, *physically*. He wanted her badly. But she was like a skittish filly and he couldn't move fast or she'd run away. This weekend would test every ounce of his patience.

He supposed it was a good thing he had something— or should he say someone—else to focus on. Namely, his brother.

"C'mon." He led Morgan downstairs and found his grandmother and parents in the family room.

"Jared, darling." His mother rose and greeted them as they approached. "I'm so glad you're here. And I assume you must be Morgan."

"Yes, ma'am," Morgan answered.

"This is my husband, Clay." His mother motioned to his father on the couch.

His father stood and came over. "Good to see you,

son." He gave Jared a handshake and rested his eyes on Morgan. He whispered. "She's a looker."

Jared grinned. "Yes, she is."

"We're so happy you could join us for a little respite," his mother gushed. "We all love it here."

"Morgan, come here." His grandmother patted the seat beside her. "Sit with me."

Jared frowned as he watched Morgan saunter over to his grandmother's side. "And what if I wanted her with me?"

"Our time with Morgan is limited, yours isn't," Ruth responded. "What do you think of the compound? My husband bought it for the family years ago."

"It's a beautiful property, Mrs. Robinson," Morgan replied. "Thank you for inviting me."

"Please call me Ruth. I still don't understand how my grandson—" Ruth glanced in his direction "—managed to catch someone as fine as you."

"Hey, hey," a deep masculine voice said from beyond the family room. Jared turned to see Chris, all six foot five inches of him, walking toward them with a petite woman with flaming red hair by his side. Jared doubted it was her natural hair color. He stood by the fireplace mantel and waited for the fireworks that were sure to come. He'd been on the receiving end of his family's discontent many times. This time the shoe was on the other foot.

"Chris! Where the hell have you been?" his father bellowed.

"Hello to you too, Dad." Chris's brown eyes rested on their father and swirled around the room. "Mama." He let go of the woman's hand long enough to bend down and brush his lips across his mother's cheek.

"It's good to see you, Chris." His mother smile was wan. Suddenly the tension in the room ramped up a notch.

Chris turned to the woman standing meekly in the doorway. She seemed afraid to enter. Had Chris told her she'd have an unwelcome audience? "Everybody? I'd like you to meet Kandi. My fiancée."

"Your what?" His mother sounded aghast.

"Have you lost your mind?" his father roared, charging at Chris. "You abandon your family and the company you've been head of—to what? Go off with and get engaged to this pop tart?"

"Clay, please," his mother said, clutching his arm. "Don't get overexcited."

"Mom's right," Chris said. "You need to calm down. We don't want you to have another heart attack."

"And who would be the cause?" his grandmother inquired. "You—for the shame you have brought to this family and our good name."

"Grandmother…" Jared said, a warning in his tone.

"No, let her go on," Chris responded. "It's exactly why I left to get away from all of this." He waved his hands in the air. "Your expectations were stifling. I couldn't breathe."

"So instead, you go to a strip club?" his father asked. "Then you get her—" he glanced at Kandi, who now stood teary eyed at Chris's side "—knocked up. For Christ's sake. And now you want to marry her?"

"I'm proud to marry Kandi. She's an incredible woman."

Ruth sighed wearily. "I had such high hopes for you, Chris. Thought you were destined to do great things. Clearly, I bet on the wrong horse. I mean, have you even looked at your brother, Jared? The one you left behind to clean up your mess."

For the first time, Chris glanced in Jared's direction.

"He's stepped up," Ruth continued. "Took over leadership at Robinson Holdings. Is dating this beautiful young woman." She motioned to Morgan at his side, who looked wide-eyed at Jared. He could see her uneasiness at having been caught in the middle of a family squabble. "I'm shocked to say this, but you could learn a thing or two from him. He's shown great resiliency these last few weeks."

Chris gave him a half smile. "If something good can come out of this, then I'm glad for it. But listen here, if any of you don't want to get to know Kandi—" he glanced around the room at their parents and grandmother "—then it's your loss. My family and I—" he placed his hand over the small swell of Kandi's stomach "—we can leave."

Jared quickly moved from the mantle and rushed to his brother's side. "Don't leave, Chris. Not like this," he murmured in his ear. "Tensions are high right now. Sleep on it."

"I don't know, bro."

"For me," Jared pleaded. "Don't go until we've talked. You owe me that much." He stared into Chris's eyes and saw him soften. At the same time, Morgan approached Kandi, and if he could have, Jared would have kissed her in front of everyone. He was so thankful for the gesture.

"Kandi, you have to see this place," Morgan said, beaming her megawatt smile. "It's an oasis. C'mon, I'll show you." He glanced over at his grandmother and saw the faint hint of a smile. Morgan had scored another goal in her favor.

But Morgan didn't need to try. She already had *him* wrapped around her little finger.

After the women departed, Jared wrapped an arm around Chris's shoulder and said, "Why don't you and I have a talk."

"Please," his father stated gruffly, "perhaps you can talk some sense into him."

Chris rolled his eyes, but allowed Jared to lead him outside onto the terrace. They were hardly through the double doors when Chris went on a tirade.

"How dare they treat Kandi like that? They don't even *know* her." Chris began pacing on the travertine deck.

"Does it really surprise you?" Jared inquired, folding his arms across his chest as he faced his brother. "Chris, you've been MIA for weeks. We had to learn via the media that you'd gotten some woman pregnant, and now you just show up and announce she's your fiancée. You didn't even have the guts to tell us the news in person. Instead, you spring this on us? It's no wonder everyone's taken aback. I am too!"

"Are you done?"

"Not nearly," Jared replied. "You've been seeing Kandi for some time. You could have introduced her to the family months ago. You're the one who chose to keep your relationship a secret as if you've got something to hide."

Chris stared at him dumbfounded. "Since when are you the voice of reason?"

"Since you left, I had no choice but to step up."

"According to grandmother, you're doing a bang-up job."

"Yeah, well, for the record, I didn't ask for this."

"Neither did I, but maybe I've been a hindrance this whole time, always bailing you out of trouble. Who knew some good old-fashioned hard work was just what the doctor ordered."

"Don't patronize me, Chris. I've never wanted to be head of the family business. That was always your forte."

"But did you ever wonder if I wanted any of it?" Chris asked. "Perhaps all their lofty expectations were thrust upon me like they were on you."

Jared looked at his brother. He'd always assumed Chris enjoyed what he did. "No, I guess I never did. Dad and Grandmother were always grooming you as the chosen one. I got a free pass."

"Lucky you," Chris said, scrubbing his jaw. "You got to enjoy life and have fun. It wasn't until I met Kandi that I finally allowed myself to let loose."

"Considering Kandi's condition, seems you let loose a bit too much," Jared responded with a chuckle.

"Hey." Chris glared at him. "Although fatherhood wasn't necessarily on my radar, I'm happy about it. Kandi's a wonderful woman and I love her."

"Whom you haven't known very long."

"Don't get on my case. Everyone is freaking out because this is the first time I've ever done anything that wasn't planned," Chris replied, walking toward Jared. When he was within striking distance, he poked Jared in the chest. "But they should really be looking at you and figuring out who this impostor is that looks like my brother."

"Funny," Jared said without humor.

"It is. Everyone's favorite good-time guy is finally doing the right thing. Go figure!" Chris said. "Is it Morgan? Is she the reason you're finally behaving like an adult?"

"That's not fair," Jared replied. "You were happy being the big brother when it suited you. And when it didn't, you ran."

"Avoidance," Chris said, laughing, "Signature Jared. You like the girl and she's good for you. Admit it!"

"She's here, isn't she?" Jared answered.

Chris chuckled. "Yeah, she is. And making a big impression on our grandmother. Apparently Kandi needs some advice on how to cozy up."

"If that's possible," Jared said, laughing. He was happy to have Chris back. He'd missed the camaraderie they shared and didn't realize how much he looked forward to their bantering.

"Since you're not going to tell me what's really going on between you and the beautiful Morgan, I'll have to find out for myself," Chris said. "Shall we go join our women?"

"Lead the way." Jared motioned for Chris to walk ahead of him.

Jared wasn't ready to tell Chris or anyone his true feelings about Morgan. How this beautiful woman was starting to capture his heart.

Twelve

Morgan had needed to do something. The Robinsons were crashing and burning around her. So she offered to show Kandi around the estate to keep the peace. Maybe Jared could smooth some ruffled feathers while they were gone. If they treated Kandi so harshly, Morgan hated to think how she would have been received if she and Ruth hadn't hit it off.

"Thank you for that," Kandi said, once they were walking back toward the house. "It was getting dicey in there."

"Ya think?" Morgan asked with a raised brow. She was surprised the woman could walk in the five-inch heels and form-fitting dress, but who was she to judge? "I'm hoping some time will help alleviate the tension."

"I doubt that's possible. Those people hate me," Kandi said, inclining her head toward the main house. "They're never going to accept me."

"You don't know that," Morgan said. "You can win them over." She opened the door to the sports pavilion, which housed the gym and basketball arena. "Check this out."

Kandi oohed and aahed like Morgan had earlier.

"It's pretty spectacular, huh?"

"Yes, and far removed from how I grew up," Kandi responded.

"Me too," Morgan murmured. "Not everyone was born with a silver spoon like Jared and Chris."

Kandi offered a small smile and Morgan hoped she was getting through to her. "So if you're not one of them, how did you win them over?"

Morgan shrugged. "I don't know. Ruth and I hit it off right away. I've never had grandparents and for some reason being around Ruth is comforting. And maybe vice versa."

"It's always been me and my mama. I was looking forward to being part of a family."

Morgan understood and wondered if that's why she felt a kinship to Kandi. She reached for Kandi's hand and gave it a gentle squeeze. "I'm new to the Robinsons too. All I can do is tell you to give it time. They'll come around."

"They won't have a choice," Chris said from behind them. He and Jared joined Morgan and Kandi on the trail. "We're getting married and having a baby."

Kandi rushed to Chris's side and encircled his waist with her arms. "True, but it would be nice if they liked me."

"All that matters is you and me," Chris murmured and bent his head to kiss her.

Morgan loved how affectionate they were. It was

clear they were in love and Morgan wanted that for herself. *Someday.* What she had right now was Jared standing there watching her from a few feet away. The heat in his gaze was unmistakable. They might not have love, but one thing was for certain: they had lust in spades.

Jared opened his arms and Morgan felt compelled to stride toward him. When he wrapped his arms around her, Morgan felt as if she'd come home.

"What do you say we give this dinner thing another try?" Jared asked.

Morgan noticed the look of absolute terror on Kandi's face. "It's okay, you have allies." She glanced up at Jared and he gave her a wink.

"We'll do it," Chris said, "but if everyone can't be civil, we're leaving."

"Let's hope it doesn't come to that," Jared responded.

The four of them walked the short distance to the main house. When they did, Antoine met them in the foyer. "Your grandmother and parents are in the dining room. They were hoping you would join them for dinner."

"Thank you, Antoine." Jared led them all down the hall.

An hour apart had allowed the older Robinsons to realize alienating Chris wasn't productive. Dinner went smoothly. Ruth played the grand hostess, though Morgan saw the tight lines around her mouth. Clay was quiet, saying only a few syllables when the conversation required it. Mary was effusive. She seemed to be the only one who was genuinely happy about Chris and Kandi's news.

"I'm so excited to plan a wedding," Mary said with a smile when the petit fours arrived for dessert. "It's going to be so much fun."

Morgan was about to tuck into hers when Chris coughed and Morgan sensed the family wasn't going to like what came next. She put her fork down on the table and waited for the fallout.

"Umm, we were thinking about just going down to the courthouse. We don't want a big fuss," Chris said.

Ruth sucked in a loud breath. "Robinsons have always been married in a church before God and family. It's a *tradition*."

"Surely a small gathering could be held at a church for the family." Morgan knew she was speaking out of turn and glanced across the table at Kandi, silently pleading for her to reconsider.

"Morgan, I appreciate…" Chris started speaking, but Kandi patted Chris's hand on the table.

"Yes, I'm sure we can work out something."

"Excellent," Ruth stated and gave Morgan a conspiratorial wink.

Morgan released a sigh, which Jared heard because he bent his head and said, "What do you say we get out of here?"

She glanced up into his dark eyes and whispered, "Are you sure?"

Jared nodded. "If you'll excuse us." He stood. "Morgan and I are going to turn in."

Morgan flushed as several sets of eyes looked at her. Were they all assuming she and Jared were going upstairs to have sex? She was sure that was the expectation, given Jared's reputation and the fact they were dating.

She allowed Jared to lead her away from the dining room, but instead of going upstairs as she'd anticipated, he said, "Walk with me for a minute."

The sky was dark but a dusting of stars could be seen as Jared took her to the outdoor living area. They walked over to a high-end wicker sectional with a large round ottoman. Jared sank down, taking Morgan with him. She settled beside him in the crook of his arm.

"Thank you for tonight," he finally said. "You were a lifesaver."

"It was nothing."

Jared peered down at her. "You and I both know it was more than that. Chris's announcement caused a mutiny in the Robinson clan. You defused the situation by taking Kandi aside so cooler heads could prevail. And I heard what you told her. You were a friend and made her feel welcome."

"Being confrontational wasn't going to solve anything," Morgan responded. "I learned from my stunt at the wedding. All it did was alienate Henry."

"You still want a relationship with him, don't you?"

Morgan's mouth ran dry and she couldn't speak; she merely nodded. "I just want to belong."

Jared turned her until she was facing him. Then he placed his hands on either side of her face. Morgan could see the heat in his gaze and something flared inside her. "You belong here with me," he murmured and then he pulled her toward him. Jared captured her mouth with his own. She kissed him back with a fervor that drew a low groan from him.

This time, they didn't pull back, and the kiss became hot and urgent as passion exploded between them. Morgan sensed a wildness in Jared he'd been holding back.

This time he didn't. He gathered her close, crushing his body against hers, and the divine fragrance of his aftershave mixed with his own uniquely male scent shot Morgan's senses into overdrive.

Jared broke the kiss and trailed kisses down her cheeks, throat and over to her neck. He lingered there and suckled. Morgan couldn't suppress the moan that escaped her lips. And she didn't stop Jared's hands when they began sliding under her sweater to cup her breasts. He teased her nipples with his thumbs until they turned into hard pebbles at his touch and Morgan wanted more.

"I'll give you more," Jared said in an amused voice. Color flared on Morgan's cheeks when she realized she'd verbalized her plea. So it was no surprise when he lifted the sweater higher and pushed aside her bra cups. Morgan felt a cool breeze against her skin seconds before he flicked his tongue back and forth across her nipple.

"Oh!" Morgan let out a cry when he continued by closing his mouth around the peak and sucking hard. Morgan sighed with pleasure as he drew her nipple even deeper into his mouth. She wasn't thinking about denying the moment. Instead, she was powerless against the tide of desire and need swelling inside her.

Jared's hands skimmed lower to her leggings and reached the apex of her thighs. She sucked in a harsh breath when he slid inside, touching her abdomen. When he came to the waistband of her panties, Morgan could feel herself blush as he brushed his hands across her. She'd never allowed another man to touch her this way, but Jared was different, so when he pushed the damp fabric to one side and touched her intimate flesh, she quivered.

"Easy, I've got you," he murmured.

His fingers teased and explored her crease and Morgan ached—for what, she didn't know. She soon found out, when he slid one finger inside and she bucked off the sectional. Jared kissed her again, this time hard and fierce, and Morgan gave herself over to the invasion of not one, but yet another digit. She writhed against his fingers as they began thrusting in and out, and lost the battle. Hot, sharp barbs of pleasure took over and her orgasm was so intense, she screamed.

Jared covered her mouth with his, absorbing her cries as his fingers continued to caress her through the waves. Morgan panted out a breath and was coming back down to earth when Jared said, "I want you, Morgan." To prove it, he brought her hand to the large swell of his erection. There was no denying how turned on he was.

But it also caused Morgan to flash back to the event in her bedroom when her mother's boyfriend Troy made her *touch* him.

"I can't!" Morgan straightened her clothes and jumped up from the sectional. "I just can't," she cried and ran as fast as she could away.

Morgan knew she was being irrational after the intimacy they'd shared, but she wasn't sure she was capable of getting over her fears, not even for Jared.

For a moment, Jared shrank backward in stunned silence. He'd never had a woman run away from him. Usually women were lining up to be with him because of his sexual prowess. But Morgan was pushing him away, and if he wasn't mistaken, tonight had been her first orgasm. She'd seemed surprised by her body's reaction to their lovemaking, but how was that possible? She was an attractive twenty-five-year-old woman. Were the men she was with incapable of pleasing her? Or was it more? He did sense a fear in her. *Had she been hurt previously in a sexual relationship?*

Was that why she was running away?

He had to know. If for no other reason than to show Morgan he could make her body hum with pleasure. Jared knew they would be spectacular together. He'd known it the minute he'd seen her at the bar at Dane's reception. He only needed Morgan to let down her guard long enough for him to show her how good it could be. She had for a moment and she'd felt so good. Tight, but good, and he couldn't wait to make love to her.

Rising to his feet, Jared gave chase.

Instead of going back to the main house as he'd anticipated, he saw Morgan skirt into one of the guest cottages on the estate. Was that a sign she wanted to be alone? Yet he couldn't let this go.

He knocked and when Morgan didn't answer, he tried the door and found it unlocked. She was sitting on a sofa in the enormous room in the gathering dark. Jared turned on the lamp on the cocktail table, giving the room a subtle glow. Morgan was squeezed onto one side of the couch as if she were going to bolt any minute. Jared sat in the chair across from her so she knew he would keep his hands off if that's what she wanted.

"What's going on, Morgan?" Jared searched her face for an answer, but all he saw were tears streaking her cheeks. "I'd like to understand what's got you so rattled. If I'm not mistaken, you enjoyed what just happened. Am I wrong?"

Morgan shook her head.

"Then was is it?" Jared asked. "Sweetheart, whatever it is, you can tell me."

Morgan sniffed and wiped away her tears with the back of her hand. When she finally looked up at him, her lashes were wet. "When I was sixteen, one of my mother's boyfriend's assaulted me."

"What!" Jared's eyes grew hard as ice. "You were raped?"

"No…" Morgan shook her head furiously. "It didn't come to that. My mother came home before—before he could."

"Morgan, I'm so sorry. You don't have to talk about this anymore."

"I have to. Don't you see?" She looked at him with beseeching eyes. "If I don't, he'll always win and keep me from having a fulfilling life."

"All right, then talk to me. What happened?"

"I came home from band practice and Troy was waiting for me. From the empty beer bottles, I could see and smell he'd been drinking."

"Go on."

"I rushed to my bedroom. He chased after me, slamming the door shut. I was terrified. He threw me on the bed and climbed on top of me. Then he was ripping my blouse open and fondling my breasts." Morgan wrung her hands and Jared's heart broke for her and all she'd been through. "He started rubbing against me. I could feel how aroused he was even though I was fighting him every step of the way. He made me touch him and told me in vivid detail what he was going to do to me. Thankfully, he heard the apartment door and jumped off me."

"What did your mother do?"

More tears fell down Morgan's cheeks. "She took his side. He told her I'd thrown myself at him and she believed him. My own mother took the word of a would-be rapist over mine!"

Jared rushed to her side and wrapped Morgan in the cocoon of his arms. "I'm so sorry, sweetheart. She was wrong. She should have believed you, *her child*."

"I always wondered if I did anything to lead him on."

"You did nothing wrong," Jared said, clutching her face in his palms. "Please tell me you know that." He wiped away her tears with the pads of his thumbs. "You didn't *deserve* what happened to you. It was your mother's job to protect you and she failed. You were the victim."

"I don't want to be a victim anymore," Morgan responded softly. "He robbed me of the joy and thrill of intimacy with a man. It's why I'm still a virgin."

Jared wasn't surprised at Morgan's bold statement. Given how skittish she was whenever things heated up between them, Jared had expected as much, but in this day and age, she was a bit of an anomaly.

"I want to take back what he stole from me and you can help me."

"I don't understand."

"Make love to me," Morgan murmured, looking up at him with her mercurial hazel-gray eyes. "Help me wash away the bad memories so all I can think about is you and how good you make me feel."

Jared shook his head. "No, I—I can't. You've been

through too much. I'm glad you were able to tell me about what happened, but I won't take advantage of you. If I did, I'd be as bad as he was."

"You're *not* taking advantage of me," Morgan replied, her tone defiant. "Back out there—" she pointed to the door "—I wanted you. Like I did that first night when I asked you up to my hotel room. I want you still. It's *my choice* to be with you."

She launched herself at him until she straddled his hips, then leaned forward and covered his mouth with hers.

For heart-stopping seconds, Jared didn't know how to respond. Morgan had been through so much and her opening up was a breakthrough. To take what she was offering tonight would be wrong, reckless even, but Morgan was pressing hot kisses all over his face and moving against him, causing his length to swell.

But she was right. It was all about choices.

And tonight, his choice was to have her.

His arms came around Morgan like steel bands and he opened his mouth to the fierce demands of her kiss.

Thirteen

A thrill rushed through Morgan when Jared responded to the passion in her kiss. Throwing herself at him was all sorts of stupid, but she hadn't known what else to do to convince Jared she was ready. He made her feel safe and cared for. She was tired of living with regrets. Desire was pulsing through her veins and she wanted to forget about anything and everything but the exquisite havoc Jared was wreaking.

His lips moved with an increasing urgency over hers, and her body came alive at the determined thrusts of his tongue. No one had ever made Morgan feel this level of excitement. When Jared crushed her against his broad chest, Morgan was left with little doubt of how strong and muscular he was. She arched into his embrace and as a result, felt the hard points of her nipples pebble against him. Jared shuddered. It gave Morgan a burst of self-confidence knowing she could stir the same emotions in him that she felt.

Suddenly Jared was lifting her off the sofa and walking. She didn't know where he was going because she was greedily kissing him. Seconds passed, then she felt the softness of the mattress as Jared laid her down and joined her on the bed. But instead of climbing astride her, he lay beside her.

"Don't stop," Morgan whispered fiercely, looking over at him.

"I have no intention of stopping. I want you, Morgan. I want to touch, taste and discover every part of your body."

Morgan's stomach dipped at his intimate words and she blushed.

"But I want you to be sure," Jared said, his dark glittering eyes laser focused on her, "so we're going to take this slow."

"I don't want slow."

Jared laughed—the low, husky sound caused every cell of her body to be acutely aware of him. "How about we undress first?"

Morgan sat up on her haunches and leaned over to start unbuttoning Jared's shirt. He smiled at her enthusiasm and seemed content to let her take over. When she was done with the buttons, he shrugged off his shirt, then deftly removed his shoes and socks and returned to the bed.

Morgan's eyes roamed over Jared's gorgeous body. He was so magnificent with his powerfully hard masculine chest and impressive six-pack. She stroked her hand down the length of his chest. Feeling the sprinkling of hair set her nerve endings on fire so she kept going until she reached the waistband of his jeans. She'd felt his lust during their kisses, but now she would feast her eyes on *him*. She unzipped his jeans, working them down his slim hips until he was able to step out of them.

Morgan's gaze dropped to his black boxer shorts, which in no way concealed his arousal. She licked her lips and slipped her hand inside the waistband to curl her fingers around him. She explored the shape of him and could feel moisture at the tip.

"Morgan." She heard the warning in Jared's tone and then his mouth was on hers in a blistering kiss sending a bolt of lightning straight through her. And when his tongue came in search of hers, she joined him in a dueling tango of lips and tongues. Jared splayed his fingers into her hair and Morgan's scalp tingled with the sensation. He was making her feel desired and every part of her wanted him.

Every part.

Jared lifted his head long enough to pull off his boxer shorts and kick them aside. Now he stood naked at the foot of the bed while she was still fully clothed. Morgan knew there was something wrong with this picture, but sensed Jared was okay with the dynamic. He was comfortable in his own skin while she was burning up.

She reached for the hem of her tunic and lifted the offending garment over her head until she was wearing only a bra. His gaze went to her breasts. Morgan reached behind her back, unclipped the bra and let the cups fall away from her breasts.

Jared swallowed audibly. "You're beautiful," he said, his voice strained. Then he moved toward her and laid her gently back down on the bed. Morgan hooked her fingers in the waistband of her leggings and glided them along with her panties down her thighs and legs, finally throwing them in a heap on the floor with the rest of their clothes.

Morgan had never gone this far with a man, never been this vulnerable. She wasn't frightened, though, because the look in Jared's eyes was naked hunger. He came down beside her and his lips found hers once more. Morgan wanted to feel his lips everywhere, tasting her and tantalizing her with sensual promise only he could fulfill. When he lifted his head at last, he was breathing hard. "You can tell me to stop at any time."

"I know, but I don't want you to."

Jared began slowly caressing her breasts. Then he lowered his head and circled his tongue around a tight nipple, teasing it. He drew the bud into his mouth with gentle sucks that sent riotous pleasure surging through Morgan. He moved his attention to the other breast and her desire ratcheted up a notch when he added teeth and gentle pressure to his ministrations.

He didn't stop at her breasts; he continued upending her with soft kisses and flicks of his tongue along her stomach and belly button. Morgan knew what came next—she'd read Harlequin romances—but she'd always she'd been too shy or embarrassed to allow what was coming next to happen.

But as Jared's mouth traveled lower, nipping the back of her knees and kissing her thighs, he stopped shy of what she really wanted. What she *needed*.

With a boldness she didn't know she had, Morgan begged. "Please…"

Jared listened.

He softly kissed her mound, allowing her time to get used to him in such an intimate part of her body. When she didn't balk, Jared gently began lapping at her with soft strokes of his tongue. The intimate caress caused powerful sensations to cascade down her body, but Morgan didn't pull away. So Jared went deeper still and when his lips and tongue came to that swollen nub, he sucked hard.

Morgan closed her eyes as Jared tantalized, licked and teased her wet core. Her heart hammered in her chest and she ached deep inside, wanting to be filled, wanting to have him inside her, but unable to voice it. Pleasure was building so hard and fast and spreading through her like wildfire and she began to shake uncontrollably.

"That's it," Jared whispered softly as her body grew tense. "Let go, so I can taste you." He continued worshiping and exploring her with his mouth. Morgan dug her nails into the tousled sheets, desperate for something to anchor her for what was coming, but there was nothing. Her orgasm was intense and she screamed out her release.

As she drifted out of the pleasure cloud, Jared was right beside her. "You okay?" he murmured.

She nodded. Blushing furiously, she tried to cover her face with her hand, but he wouldn't let her.

He framed her cheeks with his palms, his gaze searching. "Don't hide from me during our lovemaking. I need to know if you like everything we're doing or if you want me to stop. At any time, you can say no, okay?"

Tears bit at the back of her eyes. How had she found

a man so giving in the bedroom? All Morgan could do was nod.

"Good," he grinned, "because that was just the appetizer. It's time for the entrée."

Jared was doing his best to slow down—to fight his body's instinctive need to dominate and control. But he had to. Jared had never made love to a virgin, so he would have to take his time and be sure Morgan could handle each step. But it was hard on his libido—and he was hard as a rock.

He reached in the pocket of his jeans for a condom. He always carried protection though lately he'd wondered if he'd ever get the opportunity to use it. But now he knew why Morgan had been guarded. She'd been traumatized by the act of sex. It was a privilege and honor she'd chosen him to be her first partner and he didn't take it lightly. He wanted to show her how pleasurable it could be between two consenting *adults*.

He unwrapped the condom and put it on and then came back to settle between Morgan's legs, his weight propped up on his arms. "Are you sure you want to do this?"

Morgan took his face in her hands and kissed him. She wasn't tentative or scared. She deepened the kiss, entwining her tongue with his, and he tasted everything sweet and somewhat forbidden about this woman. He let her set the rhythm and pace, let her lead.

Then he reached between them and parted her with his fingers. He gently inserted one finger. When she accepted him without flinching, he inserted another, moving them ever so lightly. Morgan undulated against his hands, all the while keeping her mouth locked tightly against his. Jared loved every minute of it.

"You still okay?" he murmured, removing his hand.

"Hmm…" Morgan released a low moan.

Jared moved over her, positioned himself and slowly began to enter her, stretching her wide so she could fully accept him. He took his time so she could get used to his length.

"Oh…" Her eyes opened in wonder, locking with his.

"Am I hurting you?" Jared felt his brow crease in alarm. It was taking tremendous restraint to hold back and not thrust deep to the hilt inside her.

"No, d-don't stop…"

Jared slowly inched further inside her, inch by delicious inch. There was a moment when he reached a barrier and Morgan cried out and clutched his shoulders as she sensed the shock of his final penetration. He apologized in advance before he pushed through the last breach and was fully seated inside her.

He rose on his elbows. "Please tell me you're okay?"

"I'm fine, better than fine." Her lashes were wet, but she wasn't crying. She reached behind him and clutched his behind. "I told you don't stop."

Jared released a sigh and began thrusting, slowly and gently. He kissed her breasts and throat, taking his time on the way back to her mouth. Then he pushed his tongue between her teeth as he drove deeper inside her. Morgan arched her hips to meet his stroke.

"Yes, like that," he growled when she circled her hips, clenching her muscles around his shaft.

It felt unbelievably good to finally be with Morgan. Jared almost forgot to breathe. It was the culmination of weeks of getting to know this incredible woman who made him laugh and smile more than any woman ever had. His body screamed for him to go faster, harder. He gritted his teeth, ignoring his body's demands. Jared doubted Morgan could accept the wild untamed version of him. He had to make her first night of lovemaking one she'd never forget.

Gripping her hips, he lowered his head to suckle her breasts, first one, then the other. His body moved in circular motions and her sweet innocent body pulled him tighter and tighter. Jared didn't know how this woman could make him feel so much, but she had. He could feel his heart tightening in his chest. *What did it mean?*

Morgan sensed Jared holding back from her. She didn't know how she knew, but he was and she didn't want him to. He was her first lover and she was enjoying every minute of it, the way he felt, smelled and tasted. She was wrapping this moment up in her memory in case she never felt this way again.

"I'm not made of glass," she murmured, gripping his backside. "You don't have to be gentle."

He laughed softly and then pounded deeper, *harder.* Her hips lifted as the pressure inside her built to a crescendo. Morgan clawed her nails down Jared's back as he continued pumping. She couldn't hold anything back and suddenly let out a low, keening cry as a maelstrom of intense pleasure struck her.

Jared continued to move with an urgency and tempo that took her breath away until eventually Morgan saw stars and climaxed yet again. Then Jared emitted a low groan as shudders racked his body. *Had he experienced the same earth-shattering sensations she'd felt?*

Afterward, they collapsed in each other's arms. Morgan loved the feel of Jared's big, strong body lying on top of her and the skin-on-skin contact. His arms held her close as if he never wanted to let her go. And in this moment, Morgan didn't want him to. Because she was in love with him.

Sex wasn't clouding her brain. She'd known she was going down the rabbit hole and she'd tried valiantly to fight it, but it was too late. She was a lost cause, in love with a man who didn't believe in happily-ever-after. Yet despite knowing Jared could never return her feelings, Morgan would never regret her first time was with the man she loved.

Fourteen

Morgan slowly awoke to see dawn breaking over the clouds. She was naked, cradled against Jared's chest. She could hear his even breathing, which told her he was still asleep and she could reminisce about the previous evening.

She wasn't a virgin anymore. She was no longer the frigid woman every man told her she was. Jared had brought her alive with his kiss and his touch. She embraced the fiery attraction she'd felt. She'd never felt anything like the tumultuous fever in her flesh. Her every nerve had been activated by the act of his body becoming one with hers. She'd felt his possession deep in her inner core, and remembering it, Morgan clenched in a spasm of desire.

She felt movement beside her and realized it was the swell of Jared's morning erection. Last night, Jared had been solely focused on her; he hadn't allowed her to pleasure him. Glancing at him now, she saw his eyes were still closed, so Morgan felt a little daring. Wiggling down the sheets, she came to his engorged length. She stroked and massaged him before bringing her tongue to him and lapping with soft licks. He stirred, but didn't yet open his eyes. If he thought it was a dream, she was going to make it a good one.

Opening her mouth, she took his shaft fully inside and began moving up and down. Jared's eyes popped open and he stared down at her in stunned disbelief, but Morgan didn't let that stop her. She continued sucking him using various degrees of suction. He watched her and it gave Morgan a thrill knowing she could make him feel as good as he'd made her feel last night. But he was still fighting to stay in control, so she went to the tip and teased it with her tongue.

Jared threw his head back against the pillows and let out a guttural groan as his orgasm struck. His whole body shuddered in pleasure and Morgan continued pleasing him through the shocks.

When she was done, she glanced up at him. "So how was I?"

Jared grinned at Morgan's playfulness. When he awoke and saw himself inside her mouth, he'd nearly come right then. He'd thought he was dreaming because he'd felt hands moving over his body in an almost worshipful manner, but then those same hands grew less shy and they'd reached for his erection. She'd stroked him with confidence, making his senses go haywire. When the licks and sucks had become increasingly urgent, Jared had known it was no dream.

Who would have imagined his innocent Morgan would be pleasing him in such a way? He took her hand and kissed each one of her fingertips. "You were amazing." He knew she needed to hear it to bolster her self-confidence because he was certain she'd never done *that* to another man.

She smiled broadly. "Happy to be of service."

Jared stroked a wayward strand of hair from her face and tucked it behind her ear as he stared at her. He was usually a master at blocking any sort of feelings from getting in the way of casual sex. Being with Morgan felt much different from his no-strings flings. He'd never been involved with anyone longer than a few months, but Morgan had him crossing all sorts of boundaries. Sex with Morgan had been extremely satisfying. His attraction to her wasn't solely physical and that terrified him.

She unnerved him because she awakened something in him that up until now had been dormant. He didn't know if it was her body that had triggered something inside him, but it was there, lurking deep—the need to be close to someone and not just physically, but to tell that other person all your goals and the fears weighing you down and have them buoy you up. Morgan did that. She understood him in a way none of his casual flings ever had.

Determined to take back control, he reached for a condom and after donning it, eased Morgan back down. He brought his mouth down to hers and kissed her long and deep.

He bent his head and sent his tongue to work on her breasts. His teeth grazed one nipple in a gentle bite before soothing it with a wet flick of his tongue.

He did the same with the other, pushing it up to meet his tongue. Morgan moaned softly and he used the opportunity to move down her body with his hands until he came to her core. He gently parted her folds and used his fingertips to open her like a flower and slide inside. She gave a breathless gasp; she was still extremely tight.

He teased and tormented and when he found her sweet spot, Morgan climaxed instantly. Spreading her legs, he slid inside her with a groan. Morgan welcomed him, wrapping her legs around his hips.

"Yes, that's it," he encouraged, going deeper with his thrust. And then he moved to nibble on her neck and find the spot between her neck and ear that had her writhing underneath him.

He recognized the tension in her body and knew she was getting close. When he reached between their joined bodies and caressed her clitoris, Morgan soared, clenching around him. A pulse of pure energy went through Jared and he increased the pace with faster, deeper thrusts, which triggered his own release. He let out a ragged groan and collapsed over her.

Eventually Morgan and Jared made it out of their sex-induced coma to leave the cottage and head back to the main house. They'd fallen asleep after their dawn lovemaking session, so it was after 9:00 a.m. when they marched up the spiral staircase. Chris was descending at the same time.

"Well, well," he said with a knowing smirk. "Look who the cat dragged in. Hope you enjoyed your night." He laughed on his way down the stairs.

Morgan blushed down to the roots of her hair and

immediately rushed up the steps to their bedroom. She hoped she didn't run into anyone else who would notice they were still in yesterday's clothes. Morgan let out a deep breath when Jared closed the door behind him.

"Don't be embarrassed, Morgan," Jared said. "What happened last night is natural. My family know we're together."

"I know, but…"

Jared walked toward her, circling his arms around her. "No buts. You're my woman. Everyone expects that we're sleeping together."

Morgan laughed, looking into his gleaming dark eyes. "We weren't until last night."

"But we will be going forward," Jared said with confidence. "Because now that I've had you, I can't get enough." He bent his head and swept his mouth across hers.

Morgan pushed away from him. "Don't start something we can't finish. We probably already missed breakfast and I'm hungry."

"All right," Jared said as if he were a chastised child. "How about a shower?"

A half hour later, Morgan was embarrassed as she made her way to the dining room. She hadn't known a shower could be such a sensual experience. Jared had soaped every inch of her with a sponge, including in between her thighs, where it was a bit sore from the previous evening. Then he'd stunned her by dropping to his knees, taking one of her legs over his shoulder and pleasuring her with his mouth.

When they arrived at the dining room, it was empty

and the remnants of breakfast were being cleared by staff. They were about to leave when Antoine came in.

"Good morning." He smiled at them. "You're finally up. Would you care for some breakfast? I can have the cook whip something up."

"An omelet would be great," Morgan said, "with some veggies and whatever protein you might have. And I'd love a cup of coffee."

"Right away. Jared?" Antoine waited for a response.

"I'll have the same," Jared said, helping Morgan into her chair.

Jared sat across from her. The predatory gleam in his eye made Morgan realize he was having naughty thoughts about her. She was about to comment when Ruth stepped into the room. She was in a stylish white tennis dress and sneakers, holding a tennis racket.

"You're awake," Ruth said. "I was beginning to think you'd rather spend more time with each other than us."

Morgan was mortified and couldn't muster a response, but Jared was quick to react. "Of course not. We were just tired. If you recall I worked yesterday."

"You were tired?" Ruth smirked. "Sure, dear." She turned to Morgan. "Mary and I were about to play some tennis. Would you care to join us?"

"Um, my breakfast is coming," Morgan replied as Antoine walked in carrying a carafe of coffee. He poured Morgan a cup and moved to Jared. "Can we meet up later?"

"Of course. Get some rest." Ruth winked at Jared. "Antoine, is the court ready?" she asked on their way out, leaving Morgan and Jared alone.

Morgan's eyes were wide as she stared across the table at her lover. "She knows."

"Grandmother wasn't born yesterday. She's aware of what happens between a man and a woman who are as attracted to each other as we are."

"Is it always this—this intense?" Morgan whispered, reaching for her cup and sipping her coffee that she'd left black. She felt like she needed straight caffeine after the night they'd shared.

Jared watched her over the rim of his mug and Morgan felt a tug in her core. "Not always, but we're very compatible *sexually*."

She blinked several times, trying to escape the trance he seemed to have her in. "So what are you in the mood to do today?"

"Do I really have to answer that?" he asked with a hungry gaze.

"Jared…"

"Oh, you were talking about other than having you naked in my bed?" He placed his index finger on his chin, "Hmm, we could go hiking, canoeing on the creek or riding some horses. Whatever you want?"

"Care for some company?"

They both turned to find Chris in jeans and a polo shirt. Kandi was beside him in a denim jumpsuit looking like she was going to the club rather than a day out in the country.

"Sure." Jared eyed his brother.

"How about canoeing? You and I can race and see which of us has the biceps to win," Chris said boastfully.

"I'm game," Jared responded. "It's been a few years since I've given you a proper whipping."

"Ha, ha, we'll see who's laughing at the finish line."

Jared laughed. "Morgan and I'll meet you at the dock in about an hour after we finish up breakfast."

"See you then." Chris waved and left with Kandi.

Morgan liked seeing the brothers together. She knew the strain of not hearing from Chris had taken a toll on Jared. She was hoping this weekend would heal the rift in their family. The Robinsons weren't bad people, but they needed to be kinder to one another. Morgan supposed it was easy to see that from the outside looking in.

She could envision herself as a part of this family, but Jared didn't want a relationship with her. Once their agreement was over, they'd go their separate ways. It would be difficult because Jared was her first lover. He would always hold a special place in her heart because he'd taught her how to give and receive pleasure.

Making love with him wasn't simply about two bodies joining in mutual release. There was so much more to it than that. They'd shared an intimacy Morgan had never shared with another human being. Each kiss, each stroke, each caress had bonded her to him. She was now closer to Jared than anyone. She'd confided in him and told him all about her past. *How could she not love him?*

"Morgan?"

She glanced up and noticed Jared was frowning at her. "Is everything okay? I'd lost you for a moment."

"I'm fine."

"Fine is never good when a woman says it," Jared commented. "Are you regretting last night?"

Morgan didn't answer because Antoine came in with two steaming-hot omelets. "Thank you so much. We won't be late tomorrow and make you go through the extra work," she said.

"No worries." Antoine nodded at Jared on his way out.

Morgan was about to tuck into her food when she realized Jared was waiting on a response to his question. "No, I don't regret making love with you. It was the most wondrous, exciting experience of my life."

Jared grinned. "I'm glad. And trust me, it only gets better."

Fifteen

Jared laughed more that afternoon than he had in years. He and Morgan met Chris and Kandi at the dock as planned. After picking their respective canoes and paddles, he and Chris had helped the ladies inside. One of the groundskeepers was going to keep time and confirm the winner.

The race was challenging. Chris took off like a bat out of hell while Jared set a steady pace, conserving his energy for the long haul back. He let Chris pass him. When Morgan cried for him to move faster he said, "I've got this. Trust me."

And he did. On the return to the dock, when Chris's arms were tired and starting to fail, Jared kicked into high gear and surpassed his brother, finishing a full ten minutes ahead. He helped Morgan out of the boat, while they waited for Chris and Kandi to arrive.

"That was awesome!" Morgan yelled, wrapping her soft curves around his body and pulling him into a kiss. Jared accepted the congratulatory kiss, but he hungered for more. He had been since Morgan had cut short their shower fun earlier.

Their kiss was getting steamy so it was good thing Chris and Kandi came surging forward. "I want a recount," Chris said as the groundskeeper helped Kandi and him out of the canoe.

"I won fair and square." Jared released Morgan, but only long enough to circle his arm around her waist.

Chris rolled his eyes. "Yeah, yeah. You have youth on your side."

"Anytime you want a rematch, you need only say the word," Jared responded good-naturedly. "I'll even give you a five-minute head start."

Everyone laughed.

"How about a drink?" Chris asked wearily. "I could sure use one." He turned to Kandi and rubbed her belly. "I'm sorry, babe, it'll have to be sparkling fruit juice for you."

The group returned to the main house and found Jared's parents had returned from playing tennis. Or rather his grandmother and mother had played, while his father watched.

"There you kids are," Ruth exclaimed as she lounged on the sofa. "I was wondering if you'd abandoned us old fogies."

"Never, Grandmother." Chris pressed a kiss on her cheek and Jared was glad when she didn't pull away.

"Antoine has the chef preparing some lunch."

"I'd love some," Jared replied, joining them in the spacious living room. He and Morgan sat on one couch, while Chris and Kandi took the larger sofa with his grandmother.

"So what were you kids up to?" Ruth inquired.

"I was reminding Chris how old he is," Jared responded with a smirk.

Chris glared at him.

"They raced canoes," Kandi explained. "It was so much fun, but my pooh bear lost." She looked adoringly up at Chris.

Jared wanted to gag. He couldn't take the lovey-dovey thing. He liked Morgan a helluva lot, but he doubted he would be giving her pet names anytime soon. Even so, if he had his way, he'd have her naked for the duration of their weekend getaway. There was so much more he wanted to show her.

"I'm so glad you're enjoying your visit," his mother responded. "Ruth and I wanted to go into town and do a little shopping while the men did some fishing. We would love for you to join us so we can get to know you better."

"We would?" His grandmother raised a brow and Chris sent her a warning look.

Kandi beamed with a smile. "I would like that. I'm afraid I didn't know what to bring for a weekend retreat."

"You look great, babe," Chris said.

It was true that love was blind, Jared thought, because her denim jumper was the epitome of tacky. He was glad Morgan was a notch above the rest. She had been from the moment they'd met.

"You're coming, Morgan?" His grandmother's question was more of a statement.

Morgan didn't bother looking at Jared for reassurance. She was comfortable holding her own against Ruth. "Of course."

"Excellent."

After enjoying a leisurely lunch of seafood salad, crusty bread and pinot grigio, the women left for town while the men stayed back to go fishing. It had been a long time since Jared, Chris and their father spent any significant amount of time together. And so, after gathering their chairs, poles, tackle boxes with fishing lines hooks and baits, water bottles and much-needed insect repellant, the Robinson men headed to the creek.

Once they had their lines baited and in the water, they sat along the creek bank and waited. Fortunately, Chris was smart enough to bring a cooler full of beer, so Jared reached inside, screwed off the top and took a swig.

"I'm glad we're alone," their father began. "Perhaps now you could enlighten Jared and I how you came to be engaged to Kandi."

Chris's expression sharpened. "If you're both going to gang up on me, I'm going to head back to the house."

"Far from it," Jared said. "We just want to understand where you're coming from. How did you meet?"

Chris sighed and the tension in his shoulders slowly began to lapse. "I met Kandi after one of our clients wanted to go to a strip club. I admit it wasn't my thing, but when I saw Kandi on that stage, it was love at first sight."

"I think you're confusing lust with love, son," their father replied. "It's easy to do."

"C'mon, Jared. Don't leave me hanging. You said you met Morgan and were instantly intrigued. Am I right?" Chris asked.

"I was but that's different," Jared objected. He thought about how Chris and Kandi were already engaged. What if Morgan were his fiancée? His *fake* fiancée, he quickly amended. He couldn't offer her more than that. So why did the idea cause his heart to speed up? "Finish your story."

"After I took the client home, I came back to the club. At first, Kandi didn't want to spend time with me because I was a customer, but I convinced her to come out for breakfast. And well, the rest, as they say, is history." Chris shrugged.

"And you're sure she's not after your money?" their father inquired.

"Dad…" Jared intervened, but Clay held up his hand.

"I'm not done," he said sternly. "A young woman who's found herself on that stage may see you as her meal ticket. You're worth millions."

"Kandi isn't with me for my money. And to prove it, she's agreed to sign a prenup."

Their father rubbed his jaw. "I'm pleasantly surprised, but I'll believe it when I see it. All I'm saying, Chris, is I don't want you led around by the wrong body part. I'm shocked to say it, but perhaps you need to be more like Jared. It appears he's found a class act in Morgan. She's poised, educated and not bad on the eyes."

Jared felt proud his father thought so highly of the woman on his arm. "Thanks, Dad."

"But she is the type of girl you marry." His father wasn't short on advice. "Are you ready to handle that?"

Both Chris and his father stared at Jared, but he wasn't ready to answer their questions any more than he could the ones running through his mind since he'd met Morgan.

"How did this fishing expedition get serious all of a sudden?" Jared finally asked, lightening the mood. "I thought we were here to catch fish."

Jared thankfully got a reprieve because one of their poles moved, indicating they'd caught something. Just like Morgan had caught his heart.

Morgan had no idea part of her weekend included being mediator between the Robinsons and Kandi, but that's exactly what she was. After changing out of her active wear, Morgan donned a straight skirt, tank and her favorite jean jacket and joined the women for a jaunt into the town that was a few miles from the compound.

Ruth's version of getting to know Kandi included loaded questions destined to trip up the poor girl and have her walk into a minefield. Morgan did her best to help, but it wasn't easy. Her mind was still in the cottage with Jared where he'd introduced her to all the ways he could make her body sing.

The maelstrom of need he'd created in her after years of being frigid had Morgan feeling out of sorts. A kaleidoscope of butterflies was swirling though her insides as she anticipated the night to come with the man she loved. *But what did he feel for her?*

Kindness?

Affection?

Or was it simply about lust pure and simple.

"Morgan, darling," Ruth called to her from one of the racks in the upscale boutique where they were shopping. "You must come here. I've found the most divine dress for you."

Morgan smiled and walked over. She'd never had a grandmother. Heck, she hadn't had much of a mother, either, so being fawned over by Ruth was heartwarming. Ruth held up a stunning silk green dress, but the price tag was outrageous.

"It matches your eyes," Mary concurred.

"I'm getting it for you." Ruth handed the garment to a saleswoman who had seemed to hover nearby ever since they'd walked in.

Morgan shook her head. "I can't let you do that. It's too much."

"Of course you can," Ruth said, nodding at the clerk. "We'll take it. And you, my dear," she looked at Kandi, who'd been quiet since they'd arrived in the store, "we need to find you something."

Kandi shrugged, glancing around. "This isn't really my style."

"You mean wearing clothes with decorum?" Ruth asked.

"Ruth!" Mary called her out.

"I'm sorry," Ruth replied, "but, my dear—" she sauntered over to Kandi "—if you intend to be with my grandson, you're going to have to change your look. Because this—" Ruth motioned to Kandi's zebra-striped pants, bustier and leather jacket "—simply will not do. You will be an embarrassment to Chris and the entire family."

"Oh!" Kandi clutched her mouth and rushed out of the store.

"Ruth, did you have to be so harsh?" Morgan asked. "She's new to this world."

"So are you," Ruth responded, "but you've acclimated like fish to water. She *has* to learn proper decorum."

"And she will in time," Mary said. "I'm going to talk to her and let her know not everyone in the family shares *your* opinion."

Ruth sighed as Mary left the store. She walked over to the clerk and handed her her credit card and then turned to Morgan. "Was I harsh?"

Morgan knew Ruth respected directness so she gave it to her. "Yes, you were. Kandi doesn't have to be your enemy. In fact, you want her as your ally. Otherwise, Chris could leave again. You don't want that, do you?"

"No, of course not." She reached out and caressed Morgan's cheek with her palm. "You are a marvel. I don't know how my grandson was lucky enough to find you, but I'm so glad you're a part of this family."

Her words were like a knife to Morgan's heart, because she wasn't a part of their clan. She was only Jared's *pretend* girlfriend, but somewhere along the way it had become real. Not just for her, but for his family too. *How would they feel when they learned it was all a lie? Would they hate Morgan like they did Kandi?*

When they returned to the compound, the Robinson men were feeling very full of themselves, having caught striped and largemouth bass in the creek. While the chef was preparing their catches for the night's meal, everyone went to their respective rooms to change for dinner.

It didn't take long once the door closed to their room for Jared to reach for Morgan, but she pulled away and walked to the French doors leading to the terrace. The air outside had turned crisp and that was fine with her. She was still thinking about Ruth's comment from earlier about how Morgan had seamlessly integrated into their family. She hated lying to them, but at the time when he'd presented the offer, it had given Morgan some breathing room to figure out what came next. Because she had to face it. Henry wanted nothing to do with her. Only her siblings were interested in getting to know Morgan.

"What's wrong?" Jared asked, coming to join her outside on the terrace outside their bedroom window. He placed his arms on either side of the railing, caging her in. Morgan tried to ignore his presence behind her, but she couldn't.

It was Jared. His scent was like an aphrodisiac to her.

"I'm thinking about when this all ends."

"Don't," Jared whispered, nuzzling her neck. "Think about right now." He pulled her against him and Morgan felt the hard press of his arousal against her bottom. He lowered his head and began sucking the skin between her neck and ear he'd found was her sweet spot.

"Jared…"

"The only thing I want you thinking about—" Jared's fingers reached for the waistband of her skirt and he slipped his finger inside past the barrier of her panties until he came to her damp core "—is me inside you." He moved his hand deeper, plundering her, and Morgan felt her control slipping.

Morgan shook her head, trying to ignore the sensations coursing through her. "No, we can't. Not now. Everyone is waiting." *Were they really going to do this outside?*

"Oh we can." He shifted Morgan away from the railing and backed her up against the wall of the terrace. Before she could stop him, Jared had her plastered against his chest and was yanking her skirt up over her waist while he masterfully palmed her butt. Then he shoved his hand into her hair and gave her a no-holds-barred kiss. He literally devoured her mouth and Morgan gave up thinking about anything else except this moment.

Emboldened, she opened the button of his jeans and then the zip, until they were loose enough around his hips for her to shove them and his briefs down. Jared's erection sprang free and Morgan licked her lips. She couldn't wait to have him inside her again. Jared was quicker than she was and pulled a condom out of his pocket.

He rolled it over himself and said, "I'm sorry, Morgan, but I've been dying for you all day, so this is going to be fast and hard. I'll give you slow and sexy later."

He hooked his hand over her thigh and when he came to the thong she wore, he pushed it aside. Pinning her against the wall, Jared slid into her with one long, sure stroke. Morgan felt not only herself dissolve, but their surroundings fade away as Jared began pumping inside her.

Morgan entwined her arms around his neck and kissed him fiercely as she clutched at his shoulders. Jared continued moving his hips upward until he touched something inside her, causing her to rocket up and down against his length.

"Ride me, Morgan," Jared encouraged. "Use me."

Morgan felt her orgasm build until eventually her entire body shattered into a million pieces. Jared shouted her name as she screamed out her release into the evening sky.

Eventually, Jared let go of her thigh, but still kept her pinned against the wall. And Morgan was thankful he did because she had no strength left. Never had she felt so free and utterly abandoned.

"Was it good for you?" Jared asked with a wide grin.

"What do you think?" She smirked.

Sixteen

When Sunday afternoon arrived, Morgan was sad for the weekend to end. She'd enjoyed spending time with Jared and his family. They'd gone horseback riding that morning. It was her first time, but Ruth had insisted on buying Morgan riding breeches, a long sleeve shirt and knee-high boots during their shopping trip. Jared had barely been able to keep his hands off her in the stables as he'd helped her into the saddle.

The ride had been scenic. Even Kandi, who'd never ridden a horse either, had managed to stay upright. They'd stopped to enjoy a delicious picnic lunch of wine, chilled tiger prawns, poached lobster with tarragon, brie, baguettes and fresh fruit with Grand Marnier cream. The mood had been light and easy.

When they returned to the compound, they cooled off the horses, then everyone packed their cars to return home for the workweek ahead. Morgan hated to leave. She'd felt such a sense of belonging with the Robinsons. And it hurt, knowing it wasn't going to last.

"What's on your mind?" Jared asked as he drove her back to her apartment.

"Our arrangement will be coming to an end soon," Morgan answered.

He turned and glanced at her for a moment. "I thought I'd squashed these thoughts on the balcony. Are you that eager to be rid of me?"

Morgan frowned. "Of course not," she answered a little too quickly. When she should have been thinking of self-preservation, she'd blurted out her real feelings. The truth of the matter was, the longer they were together, the harder it would be to walk away.

"Good. Because I'm not ready for this to be over." She noticed him grip the wheel a little too tightly as he spoke.

"You're not the only one who gets a say," Morgan answered defensively.

"I know that," he murmured. "You need only the say the word and we can end it at any time."

Morgan folded her arms across her chest and stared out the window. *Was that really how Jared felt? Was she so easily expendable he'd let her go without a fight?* She knew Jared didn't do commitment, but she'd thought he felt some affection for her, if for no other reason than he'd been her first lover. Her *only* lover. She didn't want anyone else, but apparently he could take her or leave her.

And it hurt because she loved him. It was plain and simple as that, but she couldn't show her love. He would only scorn it. She had to keep her feelings hidden.

Glancing around, Morgan noticed that Jared had missed the turn to the Residences at the W. "Where are we going?"

"To my place," he said, looking straight ahead.

She couldn't go home with him. If she did, Morgan was afraid of what she might reveal. "Jared, it's been a long weekend and you have to work in the morning. I think it's best if I go home."

He glanced at her, but his eyes were hooded. "I'd rather you came home with me, but if you want me to turn the car around, I will."

Morgan swallowed. He was putting the decision in her hands. Or was he really? *Was this some sort of manipulation to get her to do what he wanted?* Whatever the reason, deep down Morgan wanted to be with him. "Fine."

Conversation was nonexistent for the remainder of the drive and on the elevator ride up to his penthouse. Once inside, Jared placed their luggage on the floor and turned to her. "I'm sorry."

Morgan stared at him in disbelief. Jared wasn't a man who apologized. He was cocky, arrogant at times, but always self-assured. But when she looked at him his expression was uncertain. *Had he never told someone sorry before?*

"Why are you sorry?"

"For what I said earlier," Jared explained, shifting from one foot to the other. "Or should I say the callous way I said it. We have something good and I don't want it to end. There, are you happy now?"

Morgan smiled. "That you apologized?" she asked, coming toward him. Despite her brain screaming to run for the hills, she wound her arms around his neck.

"No. That you got me to admit my feelings," he responded.

"A little humble pie never hurt," Morgan said, looking at him from under her lashes. "So why don't you get to apologizing." She grabbed him by the head and planted her lips on his.

The next morning, Jared sat in his office at Robinson Holdings staring at his laptop. He'd been looking at the same set of figures for an hour and they still made no sense. His mind kept wandering to when he'd kissed Morgan awake near dawn. He'd ignored her protests for sleep and nudged her legs apart with his shoulders.

Pressing his mouth against her feminine core, he'd feasted on her sweetness until he heard her moans of pleasure. He hadn't been satisfied with just a taste. Instead, he'd turned her over onto her stomach and taken her from behind. He'd fondled her breasts while thrusting inside her and teasing her wet sex until she'd screamed his name. Only then had Jared been sated enough to drift off to sleep.

The problem was that sex wasn't just sex with Morgan. It was a discovery of all the secret ways he could pleasure her. Jared was toying with the idea of extending their relationship even though he'd already convinced his grandmother of his committed status but the board was still skeptical, so he needed to keep up appearances. He kept telling himself it was all about sex.

Great sex.

He didn't want or need the fairy tale Morgan undoubtedly wanted. He didn't do commitment of any kind. So why was he doubting everything he'd ever told himself?

"It's really strange seeing you behind that desk," Chris said from the doorway.

Jared was surprised to see his brother in a gray suit and tie standing on the threshold of his office. *Chris's former office.*

"It feels strange for me too," Jared responded. "What brings you by?"

A disconcerted look came across his brother's features. "Well, I…"

"You thought now that you've returned, Jared would step aside?" their grandmother inquired from behind him.

Chris instantly jumped at the sound of her voice. "To be honest," Chris replied, "yes. I thought Jared would relish the opportunity to get back to his former lifestyle of laid back days and fast nights."

"Those days are over now that he's met Morgan," Ruth answered. "He wouldn't ruin that by reverting to his former playboy ways."

Jared noted the look of disbelief on his brother's face.

"It might surprise you, Chris, but I have enjoyed learning more about Robinson Holdings and I don't intend on leaving." Jared shocked himself by agreeing with their grandmother.

"What am I supposed to do?" Chris asked.

Jared rose to his feet and buttoned his suit jacket. "We can share the responsibilities. As you said, one person handling all the weight is *too* much. We can share."

"I don't think I agreed to that," their grandmother interjected, folding her arms across her chest. "And nei-

ther did the board. You've begun to gain their grudg-
ing respect, Jared. Why stop now?"

"Because I want to have a life, Grandmother." Jared
didn't know if that included or didn't include Morgan,
but he would never find out if he walked the same path
as Chris. "I don't want to burn out like Chris did. No
offense." He glanced at his older brother. "You must
see this is the best solution. And I need your help in
convincing the board."

She stared at him. "I have to say, Jared, you've impressed me these past weeks and I'm really proud of
you."

Jared grinned. "Thank you."

"So am I." Chris faked a sniff and they both laughed.
"I would be honored to work with you, brother." He offered his hand and Jared shook it.

"It was so nice of you to join me," Kandi said when
she and Morgan met up midweek at a baby boutique
frequented by upper class moms. Morgan had been
surprised to receive the invite, but suspected Kandi
needed a friendly ear.

"No problem," Morgan replied. "I'm happy to help."

"I'm nervous," Kandi said as she ran her fingers
over the blankets. "Not about having the baby, about
fitting into Chris's family. You seem to be such a hit
with his parents and grandmother. I was hoping you
could give me some pointers."

"Be yourself," Morgan said evenly. "Ruth is all fire,
but once you get to know her, there's a warm individ-
ual underneath."

Kandi gave her an incredulous look and Morgan
couldn't resist a chuckle. "Okay, maybe warm is push-

ing it, but I don't know…we sort of hit it off. She's like the grandmother I never had."

"A cranky one. She criticized everything I wore this weekend."

Morgan lowered her head.

"What?" Kandi asked, putting her hands on her expanding hips. She was in leopard print pants, a bodysuit and bomber jacket.

"If you want to fit in, you have to dress the part. I'm not saying you have to lose your individuality. Just tone it down a notch. Not so many low-cut tops, skintight jeans or leopard prints."

"That's how I got Chris," Kandi said with a smirk.

"But it won't be how you'll keep him. I can help you find a few things that you can sprinkle in with your own clothes. How's that sound?"

Kandi shrugged. "If you say so, but I think I look fabulous."

Morgan smiled. Kandi would think that, but the mirror was lying to her.

Later that evening, after enjoying takeout over a bottle of wine, Morgan regaled Jared with stories of her day with Kandi. Morgan liked that they could sit in their comfy clothes on the sofa like a real couple and have a night at home. She was in a tank top and yoga pants while Jared wore a T-shirt and sweatpants.

"You don't have to hang out with her if you don't want to," Jared responded. "It's not a condition of being my girlfriend."

Morgan frowned, feeling a bit annoyed. "I know that, but I like Kandi. She reminds me in many ways of my mother. Misguided. I thought I could help her win over your grandmother." Then she paused to stare at him for a moment. Did he realize he'd called her his girlfriend? Not his pretend one?

Jared looked at her incredulously. "That's not likely, Morgan. Don't go giving Kandi false hope."

"C'mon, she's not that bad."

"No, but once my grandmother forms an opinion, it's hard to convince her otherwise."

"You did," Morgan responded, poking him in the chest. "In a short time, you've been able to convince Ruth of your willingness and ability to lead Robinson Holdings. Surely, Kandi can change her mind, too?"

"I'm her grandson. I'm family."

"I refuse to believe that's all it's about," Morgan replied. "With a little grooming and maybe some etiquette classes, Kandi can overcome…" She searched for the right words.

"Her lack of class?" Jared offered.

"That's harsh."

"But true. Don't go changing Kandi. Chris fell in love with her exactly as she is. They'll have to muddle their way through this."

Morgan lowered her lashes. "I'm sorry. I was only trying to help."

"Aw, come here," he murmured, reaching over to pull her into his lap. "You didn't do anything wrong. It was a really nice thing to do. And I…" He stopped midsentence and without another word, lifted her away from him and rushed out of the room, leaving Morgan wondering exactly what he'd been about to say.

Jared splashed water over his face in the master bath. *What the hell?* He'd almost said, "And I love that about you." *Love*. That word wasn't in his vocabulary when it came to any other woman. So why now?

It was Morgan.

She made him feel.

For the first time, a woman had stumbled into his life and he'd forgotten to put up barriers to keep her out and his emotions in. With Morgan, Jared's feelings were allowed free reign and he didn't know how to coral them back in.

A knock sounded on the door.

"You okay?" Morgan inquired from the other side. "The way you got up so fast—I hope it wasn't something we ate?"

Of course she would think it was food poisoning rather than him running away because he was scared of the emotions she was bringing to the surface.

"I'm fine. I'll be out in a second."

"Okay." He heard her retreating footsteps and sucked in a deep breath.

He'd thought he could have it both ways, that he could keep Morgan and not get caught up. But he was wrong. He wasn't the settling down kind. Never had been. Never would be. Morgan deserved a man who could give her his whole heart and who knew how to love. He wasn't that man. He had to let her go.

His hands gripped the countertop. But how could he deny the attraction they shared? He'd never met a woman he'd wanted so much. When Morgan was in his arms, his entire body felt electric. It had been that way from the start when he'd noticed her at the wedding reception. He'd instantly wanted to claim her as his own as he did now. Thinking about her made him want to get them both naked.

Jared stood straight.

One more night. That was all he would give himself. Maybe then, he could find a way for them both to move on.

But the minute he came out of the bathroom, Jared found Morgan sprawled across his bed, naked, wearing nothing but a smile. All thoughts of saying goodbye to this gorgeous woman flew out the window as hot, molten lust drove him to fling off his T-shirt, drop his sweats and briefs and charge toward the bed.

He allowed himself enough time to don a condom before slanting his lips over hers in a demanding kiss that sent his pulse racing. Morgan responded by teasing her tongue with his own. Jared reacted by covering her body with his and smoothly thrusting inside her.

Incredible pleasure coursed through Jared and he wanted to close his eyes, but he couldn't. He wanted to look up at Morgan because who knew if this might be the last time they were together. Their eyes locked and Morgan lifted her hips to move with him in unison until a tidal wave of passion swept over them and they both exploded. Jared saw stars as he continued pumping the last of his release. With their sweaty bodies entwined together, Jared fell asleep in Morgan's arms.

Seventeen

"Thank you so much for agreeing to meet me, Fallon," Morgan said when her sister joined her at the downtown wine bar the following evening. She'd dressed casually in black jeans, ruffled shirt and ankle booties. Fallon was equally relaxed in gray slacks, a lavender silk shirt and flats after coming straight from the Stewart Technologies offices.

Morgan needed someone to confide in about her feelings for Jared. Although she liked Kandi, their relationship was still so new. Morgan didn't feel like she could pour her heart out to Kandi.

"I was happy to get the call." Fallon leaned back against one of the sofas in the corner of the room and sipped from her wineglass. "I was hoping one day you'd feel comfortable enough to consider me not just a sister, but a friend."

"I feel like I need one."

Ever since she and Jared had shared takeout and acted domestic like a real couple a few nights ago, he'd been acting distant. She hadn't seen him all week. He'd told her he had to work, but Morgan felt like it was an excuse.

Had she done something wrong?

Had the novelty of being with a virgin her first time worn off?

She wouldn't have thought so, because it appeared he'd been satisfied after they'd made love, but what did she know?

"Talk to me," Fallon said, leaning in. "What's going on?"

"I'm sure you've heard I've been seeing Jared Robinson." Morgan took a sip of her crisp Riesling.

Fallon nodded. "I was surprised anyone would be 'seeing Jared.'" Fallon made air quotes with her fingers. "He's always been a sly one with the ladies."

"I know." Morgan offered a small smile. "His reputation precedes him."

"That's an understatement." Fallon chuckled. "You have no idea the amount of mayhem he and Dane used to get into."

"He told me before he asked me to be his pretend girlfriend."

Fallon sat up straight. "Pretend girlfriend?" She frowned. "Explain."

Morgan filled Fallon in on the details of their deal, explaining Jared's predicament with the board, his grandmother's demands and Chris's absence.

"Morgan, honey." Fallon reached for her hand, "You didn't have to do this. Ayden and I, even Dane would have helped you find a job or given you whatever you need."

"After Henry's rejection, I was determined to make it under my own steam without any help from the Stewarts. That's why I accepted the offer. But then Jared and I started spending time together and I realized I liked him."

Fallon raised a brow.

"I think I love him, Fallon," Morgan said quietly, glancing at her sister. "And if I'm honest, it might have been love at first sight when he rescued me at the wedding after I'd humiliated myself in front of our father. I drank too much and threw myself at him, but he didn't take me up on it. Instead, he put me to bed when I got sick."

"As he should have done," Fallon responded hotly.

"Hey, it's not his fault," Morgan said. "He was very clear about our arrangement. Except somewhere along the line, our relationship became more intimate."

"And you slept with him?"

Morgan nodded. "You see—it was the first time I'd ever…" She couldn't go on. It was too embarrassing at her age to reveal she'd still been a virgin.

"Been with a man?" Fallon picked up on what Morgan hadn't been able to say aloud. "Did Jared take advantage of you? If he did, I'll sic Dane on him."

Morgan shook her head fiercely. "No, I wanted him and it was wonderful. He was patient and gentle. And since then, well, it's been nothing short of amazing. Or at least I thought it was. But the last few days, I can feel Jared pulling away."

"And you're worried he's lost interest?"

"Yes."

"Oh, sweetie, these things happen. Sometimes we're not always meant to be with our *firsts*. Sometimes they're only meant for right now. And considering Jared's background, distance could be his way of trying to end your relationship without coming right out and telling you."

"I don't want it to end." Tears seeped out of Morgan's eyes and she wiped them away with her fingertips. "I love him."

"Have you told him?"

She shook her head.

"Has he said those three little words to you?"

"No."

"I don't want to hurt you, but a guy like Jared isn't meant for the long haul. He's not the marrying kind."

Morgan knew Fallon spoke the truth, but to hear it out loud still hurt. Perhaps she'd needed someone to sound the alarm and snap her out of this fantasy she'd been living in where she and Jared had a happy ending.

"Come here." Fallon wrapped Morgan in her embrace and Morgan softly sobbed in her big sister's arms. "I know it seems like the end of the word now, but I promise you, you'll get through this."

Morgan wasn't sure. *How did you get over your first love?*

Morgan heard from Jared later that evening. She was at her apartment getting ready for bed and was curled under the cover with a good book when he finally called.

"Hello."

"Morgan, I'm sorry I've been MIA this week," Jared said.

"I understand. You've been busy." She didn't understand, not after the intimacies they'd shared, but what else could she say? She wasn't about to embarrass herself by appearing needy and desperate for his company.

"I know it's short notice, but I forgot to tell you about a charity event on Saturday my grandmother throws every year. It's for Alzheimer's research. It would mean a lot if you could come with me."

Damn him.

Right when she was ready to write him off, Jared sprang this on her. She wanted to say hell no, she wouldn't go. A girl had to have some pride. Yet despite his lack of interest in her over the past week, he had to know she wouldn't turn him down knowing how dear this cause was to him.

"Morgan?"

She blinked and realized it had been several moments since he'd asked the question. "Yes?"

"Will you go?"

She paused again. Her head told her to end this now while she still could, but her heart told her to be there for the man she loved even knowing how much it might cost her in the end. "Yes, I'll attend."

She heard his audible sigh of relief on the other end. "Thank you. It's black tie, so buy whatever you need."

"I'll do that."

"All right, well, I'll pick you up on Saturday night around six. Sound good?" His voice was stilted as if he was finding the conversation as difficult as she was. *How could two people be so close one moment and so far apart the next?*

"Fine."

"Okay. Well…have a good night." Seconds later, he'd hung up.

Morgan's heart sank when Jared ended the call so quickly. He couldn't bear to talk to her when barely a week ago, he couldn't keep his hands off her? *Was she really so terrible he no longer wanted her?*

Morgan threw the phone down and flung herself on bed. This mess was of her own making. She'd agreed to this arrangement, which was supposed to be strictly platonic. Instead, she'd let herself be drawn into Jared's family life and into his bed and now she was in too deep to see a way out.

Jared stared at the handset on his desk in his office. He felt horrible. He'd been cold and distant with Morgan and she didn't deserve it. She hadn't done anything wrong. She'd done everything he'd asked of her. No, she'd done more. She'd endeared herself to his grandmother and his entire family loved her. She'd befriended Kandi when she didn't have to.

As for him, she'd brought a happiness into his life he hadn't known before. He smiled. Laughed. And it was all because of Morgan. *She* was turning him into a better man. He was more engaged in his life than he'd ever been. It was no longer about the women, fancy cars and extravagant trips.

Having Robinson Holdings thrown into his lap had forced him to grow up and take stock of his life. He'd been going through the motions for years, aimlessly rushing from one thing to the next with no real direction. Becoming CEO had shown Jared he was not a useless member of the family. He had value and brought something to the table other than a bad boy reputation.

Meeting Morgan was the other catalyst. Seeing her at Dane's wedding had revealed a protective side of his nature. He'd never considered himself a knight in shining armor by any stretch of the imagination, but somehow because of Morgan he'd become one. Saving her from the leech who'd been manhandling her at the wedding. Taking care of her when she'd become ill in her hotel room and putting her to bed. Stopping her from blowing up her family's reputation with the gossip blogger. He'd done all of those things because *she* brought out the best in him.

Then their relationship took a turn at his family's compound as he'd always known it would. The attraction between them was too strong to be denied. She'd opened up to him about her past and allowed him the special gift of being the first man to make love to her. And it had been epic. Beyond his wildest dreams or anything he could ever have imagined.

She'd *touched* him.

Now he was acutely aware of her—whether it was the inflection in her voice, the scent of her hair or the fit of those skinny jeans she loved to wear. He had spent every night of the last week lying awake, recalling their passionate unions, and he'd literally ached. All of it disarmed him and he didn't know how to deal with it. He knew how to be the man he'd been, but Jared wasn't sure he could give her the white picket fence she inevitably wanted. This week he'd pushed her away in hope of getting her out of his head. Or was it his *heart* he was afraid of?

Avoidance had worked until Ruth reminded him of the charity event she held every year in his grandfather's honor to raise awareness about Alzheimer's and find a cure. He was ashamed to say it, given how he'd treated Morgan all week, pretty much ignoring her, but he *needed* her there. Not just for his grandmother, but for *him*. Every year, the event got harder and harder because his grandfather was slipping further and further away. Jared couldn't stop it or control the outcome.

Morgan's presence would be a balm; a comfort on a night when he needed it most. Jared knew he was being unfair. He should end it so Morgan could find someone worthy of her love and affection. He suspected she had feelings for him and it gutted him because he *couldn't* return them.

Somehow, he would get through the night. And when it was over, he would release her from their arrangement. *What choice did he have if he wasn't willing to commit?*

Eighteen

The night of the charity event, Morgan reminded herself to be calm, cool and collected. She mustn't get carried away by the grandeur of being on Jared's arm because after all it was a mirage.

When Jared arrived to pick her up from her apartment, he'd been distant. He'd remarked on how beautiful she looked in the shimmery metallic Dior gown with spaghetti straps she'd purchased earlier that day. The top was a bustier style, and the skirt, covered with thousands of silver sequins, flowed all the way to the floor. Morgan had loved the dress instantly despite the outrageous price tag.

She'd chosen to wear her hair down tonight and it now hung in luxurious waves down her back. Between the salon and the store, she'd had little time to get ready so she'd had to apply her own makeup. She was pleased with her appearance until she encountered Jared's lackluster reception. He, on the other hand, looked dashing in a tuxedo, and it made Morgan's heart clench in her chest.

She sat as far from Jared as she could in the limousine he'd hired. She couldn't bear to look at him, let alone touch him, because deep in her gut, Morgan knew what they had was over.

The event was being held at the Hotel Ella, a beautiful historic hotel with a large wraparound veranda, circular staircase and expansive front lawn. Morgan half expected Scarlett O'Hara to descend the steps as they entered the foyer.

Scarlett didn't, but Ruth Robinson greeted them in a floor-length gown and swept her up in a hug. "My darling, you look stunning." She stroked Morgan's cheek and turned to her grandson. "Doesn't she, Jared?"

He looked at Morgan and the arresting expression in his eyes caused her to nearly stop breathing. She hadn't seen that look all week and she hated that it still mattered to her. Morgan accepted a glass of champagne from a passing waiter, swigged it and set it back on the tray.

"Yes, she does," Jared responded.

Jared's parents came forward to greet Morgan as did Chris and Kandi. Chris looked handsome in a navy tuxedo while shockingly Kandi wore a simple strapless gown with a side slit. It was tasteful and elegant. She was finally listening to Morgan's advice and it brought a smile to her face. It reminded Morgan of how in a short time, these people had come to mean a lot to her.

"C'mon, I'd like to introduce you around." Ruth looped her arm through Morgan's and led her away.

Morgan was thankful for a reprieve to get her mask back in place. She couldn't let Jared know how much he was hurting her with his coldness.

"Is everything all right, my dear?" Ruth asked, once they were some distance away.

Morgan offered a small smile. "Everything's fine."

Ruth raised a brow. "What's going on? Has my grandson done something wrong I need to give him a kick in the shins over?"

"No." It wasn't Ruth's business what went on between her and Jared. She couldn't put her in the middle and certainly wouldn't cause dissension in the family now that their relationships were on better footing.

"All right, well, if you need me. I'm here," Ruth said and walked over to a small group in the corner. "Everyone, I'd like to introduce you to Morgan Stewart. She's my grandson's girlfriend and very dear to me."

Several pairs of eyes landed on Morgan. What she hadn't been expected was to see her father and Nora in the group. Morgan swallowed the lump in her throat. She prayed neither of them would make a scene.

She needn't have worried because Henry looked through her as if she wasn't there and Nora, well, she x-rayed Morgan as if she was a specimen on a slab. She stared incessantly for what seemed like an eternity. Nora must have found her wanting, because she immediately excused herself. Henry glared at Morgan and quickly moved away to follow his wife.

Morgan tensed. Henry didn't need to speak to relay the message. He hated her. "If you'll excuse me, I'm going to go powder my nose." She extricated her arm from Ruth's and quickly walked away. She was moving through the ballroom, trying to keep the tears at bay when a figure moved into her path.

"Morgan, are you all right?"

She heard Jared's voice, but she wanted nothing to do with him. Not now. She needed air. Morgan rushed out and through a haze of tears she saw the sign for the restroom. She passed a varied collection of contemporary art until she arrived at a luxuriously appointed ladies' room complete with a sitting room.

Morgan sank into one of the chairs and reached for a Kleenex sitting on the nearby table. Why did *he* have to be here? Morgan wondered. She could have gotten through the night and Jared's coldness toward her, but to see the father who refused to acknowledge her was too much. Even hearing she'd taken his name hadn't elicited a reaction from Henry. Just fury.

Tears flowed down her cheeks. *Why was she here and putting herself through this abuse?* She should have left Austin as soon as Henry rejected her. Instead, she'd allowed herself to get caught up in Jared's life. And now that he'd gotten what he wanted, Jared was done with her.

"Really? You're going to cry now after everything you've done?"

Morgan glanced up into the stormy brown eyes of Nora Stewart. She wore a long red gown with a V neckline and a billowing skirt. She looked regal and every bit the queen of the ball. Morgan sat up straight. "What do you want?"

"I want you to go back to whatever rock you crawled out from under and leave my family alone. You have no place here."

Morgan stared at Nora and that's when she realized

it. Nora knew she was Henry's daughter because tonight, for the first time, she'd *really* looked at Morgan and seen the same eyes staring back at her. "I have every right to be here. I'm Henry's daughter."

"You're a mistake," Nora said. "A moment of weakness on Henry's part."

Nora admitted the truth! "And you've forgiven him for cheating on you?" Morgan asked incredulously. "Why?"

"Despite what everyone might think of me, I love Henry and we've spent a lifetime together. I won't let an interloper come in and cause friction in my family."

Morgan rose to her feet. She wasn't going to let Nora intimidate her. "They're my family too. I didn't ask for any of this."

"Yet, here you are making pronouncements at Dane's wedding. Showing up on our doorstep with your hand out," Nora responded, folding her arms across her chest. "What else am I supposed to think?"

Morgan sighed. "I admit I could have waited for a more opportune time, but I didn't know if Henry would see me, let alone believe me. And guess what? He didn't. He hates me as much as he hates Ayden."

Nora sighed. "Henry doesn't hate you, but seeing you is like seeing his failure, his mistakes all over again."

"I'm not a mistake," Morgan said fiercely.

"You must see you're not going to get the result you're looking for. Henry will never accept you. Isn't it better that you move on from this town? Hooking yourself up with Jared Robinson, a notorious playboy, will only bring you heartache."

"Leave my relationship with Jared out of this."

"How can I? When you've flaunted it to all of Austin," Nora said, sweeping her hand wide. "He'll never marry you. I've known that young man since he was a child and he's easily bored, moving on to the next thing before he's put down the first. You're merely a distraction, nothing more."

Morgan's eyes narrowed. Even if Nora's words struck a chord, she would never let her see it. "You can keep your observations to yourself."

Nora shrugged. "Don't say I didn't warn you." Lifting her skirts, she swept out of the room, leaving Morgan staring after her.

Once she was gone, Morgan crumbled into the chair and placed both her hands over her face. Tonight was an epic fail. Not only had Jared rejected her, but so had her father. And according to Nora, that wasn't ever going to change. She was a "mistake." Whenever he saw her, Henry was reminded he'd cheated on his wife and she was the result. She was unwanted by every man in her life.

She had to leave now with as much dignity as she could muster. Rising to her feet, she rushed over to the sink and tried to repair the damage her crying jag had done to her makeup. She managed to obscure it, but her eyes were still red and rimmed with pain. Breathing deeply, Morgan pulled out her cell and called for an Uber. The car was nearby and would be there in minutes. She intended to slip out quietly before anyone else saw her.

Morgan prepared to move swiftly down the corridor but Jared was leaning on the wall outside the restroom. He stood upright when he saw her.

"Morgan?" He rushed to her side and tried to touch her cheek, but she moved away.

"Don't touch me!"

"What happened in there?" Jared didn't let her harsh tone deter him. "What did Nora say to you?"

Morgan didn't answer. She started down the hall. As she did, a young woman stepped in front of her to block her way. Morgan recognized the redhead. It was Ally, the journalist Morgan had tried to sell her story to.

"Morgan Stewart?" she said. "We meet again."

"Excuse me." Morgan tried to step away, but Ally moved in front of her.

"Not so fast," Ally replied. "I wish I had stuck around. You had a story to tell me and I should have listened. How was I to know you were Dane Stewart's baby sister? But it doesn't matter. I've got the local scoop. You've been seeing Jared Robinson, Austin's most notorious bachelor."

"I have no comment." Once again, Morgan tried to leave, but Ally wasn't budging. "Please step aside."

"You might not want to confirm your relationship with Jared, but perhaps you might want to comment on my latest story. Seems Jared here has a love child with his former fling Samantha Russell whom he's left to languish in poverty. Do you have a comment on that?"

"A child?" Jared roared from behind Morgan. "You must be out of your mind, Ally. I knew you liked to make up stories, but that's utter rubbish."

Morgan's stomach lurched. "Is it?" she asked, spinning around to face him.

Ally smirked at seeing her handiwork. "Jared has a child, Morgan. Didn't he tell you? Do you have a comment *now*?"

"I have to go." This time, Morgan shouldered past the woman and rushed down the corridor. She didn't stop until she reached the outside and had run down the steps. Glancing around, she saw the car with an Uber sign in the window. Rushing toward it, she was nearly to the door when Jared caught up with her.

Jared grabbed her arm and spun her around. "Morgan, please, don't leave like this."

The desperation in his eyes was evident, but Morgan didn't care. "Please, let me go."

"I can't do that," Jared said. Concern was etched across his handsome features. "Not like this. I can't let you leave thinking the worst of me."

"Why should that matter to you, Jared?" She tugged on her arm and he released her. "You've ignored me all week. And tonight, I came here for *you*. Yet you treat me like something on the bottom of your shoe. Just like my father. I won't take it. Not anymore. I deserve better."

"Morgan…"

"Don't apologize. I agreed to this arrangement. It was temporary and I accept that. But a child? For Christ's sake, how could you abandon your own child?" Shaking her head in disbelief, she reached for the door handle and slid inside the car, but Jared blocked her from closing it.

"She's lying, Morgan. I would never abandon any child of mine, ever. If you believe nothing else from our time together, believe that."

He let go of the door and Morgan slammed it shut. "You can go to hell!"

The driver drove away and Morgan's last view was of Jared staring after the car with sadness in his eyes.

It was over between them and finding out Jared abandoned his child was further confirmation that Morgan
walking away was the best decision she'd ever made.

Nineteen

He let her go.

He shouldn't have. The despair in Morgan's eyes destroyed Jared. He'd been keeping her at a distance all week, including tonight. In his mind, he'd done it for her own good, but he hadn't wanted to hurt her. Yet he didn't think he was good for her either. On the other hand, he wasn't the monster Ally was claiming he was.

Hearing the car door click shut was like a vault slamming, shutting him out of something so precious, Jared knew he'd never get it back.

"Jared, what is this I hear about you fathering a child? My God what's happening in this family? First Chris and now you?" His grandmother confronted him once he returned to the ballroom. The look on her face wasn't embarrassment, it was disappointment.

He hadn't seen her expression of chagrin aimed at him in weeks and realized he never wanted to see it return.

"It isn't true."

"Are you sure about that?" His parents came over and his father was the first to jump on the bandwagon. "Up until Morgan, you were quite the playboy."

Chris and Kandi joined their circle and his brother defended him. "Jared would never be that negligent. There's one thing Jared has always practiced and that's safe sex."

"Must you be so crude, Chris?" his mother scolded.

"I will repeat. I don't have a child," Jared said, rather loudly so that several people standing nearby glanced up at his raised voice. "And I certainly wouldn't leave one I'd fathered to be raised without me. I'll prove it to all of you. To the entire world if I have to."

His mother breathed a sigh of relief, but his father still looked skeptical. Jared glanced at his grandmother. "Please tell me you believe me, Grandma?" He'd never called her that, but the endearment came to his mind given how close they'd become in recent weeks.

She didn't reply. Instead, she glanced around the room. "Where's Morgan?"

Jared lowered his head.

"Where is she?"

"She's gone," he answered.

"Because she believes this story?" his grandmother asked. "If your girlfriend believes this is true, how can we not?"

"She's not my girlfriend," Jared blurted out.

His grandmother frowned. Jared glanced around; his entire family looked perplexed. "What do you mean, son?" his father inquired.

It was time to come clean. He was tired of the secret. "I asked Morgan to pretend to be my girlfriend to help win over grandmother and the board."

Several looks of disbelief came his way. Even Chris rolled his eyes upward and spoke quietly to Kandi, who stepped away from the group so the Robinsons could have some privacy. "What the hell did you do, Jared?"

"I don't believe it." His grandmother shook her head. "What I saw between you wasn't make-believe. Morgan cares for you. I would bet my life on it."

Jared lowered his head. "She probably does, but I don't deserve her. She's too good for me."

"Why would you deceive us?" his mother asked. He could see that for once, he'd exasperated even her.

Jared sighed. "I didn't set out to lie to you. I just wanted to prove to everyone I could be like Chris and run the business." He motioned to his brother, who was scraping his jaw with his hand. "That I could step into his shoes. Grandmother said the board would prefer someone settled so I…" His voice trailed off.

"Roped Morgan into your lies," his grandmother finished. "How typical. And now she has feelings for you, but you've gotten yourself caught up in a scandal. My God, Jared, when will you ever learn?" Turning on her heel, she stormed away.

She wasn't the only one. His parents expressed their disappointment in him once more before heading off, leaving Jared and Chris alone. Jared was glad his brother didn't leave him and was still at his side as he'd been so many times.

"Well, you've really done it this time," Chris said.

Jared glared at him. "Yeah, I know. I've mucked it up bad. What am I going to do?"

Chris wrapped an arm around his shoulder. "The first thing you're going to do is clear your name of this slander about the baby. And then, you're going to get your woman back."

"Morgan?" Jared shook his head. "I can't. That ship has sailed. She thinks I fathered a child and abandoned it like her father did her. We're done."

Except Jared didn't feel like they were over.

"You have to talk to her," Chris said. "Convince her of the truth. I've seen you with Morgan, Jared. You're a different man—dare I say, a better man—because of her. You need Morgan. You have to make this right."

Jared nodded. He doubted Morgan would open the door to him, let alone listen to a word he had to say. He may have hurt her so bad that there was no coming back from it, but he wouldn't know unless he tried.

Morgan was on autopilot. She had been since last night when somehow she'd made it from the Uber to her apartment. Once the door shut, however, she'd fallen to the floor in a heap, where she'd stayed until she was all cried out. Eventually, she went to her bedroom, where she'd drawn the shades, curled into bed and turned off her phone. She needed sleep.

Except her sleep wasn't peaceful. She dreamed of Jared's smile. His laugh. His sinful abs. His tight butt, which she'd grasped as he'd driven her to the brink of pleasure. But that was over. It had been an illusion. A lie.

Jared wasn't the man she thought he was. He'd turned his back on her like he'd done his own child. He was no better than Henry. And she'd fallen head over heels in love with him. What a fool she'd been to fall for his lies hook, line and sinker.

She drifted off to sleep near dawn. When she woke up, Morgan had a plan: get out of Austin. She would go someplace remote to clear her head so she could figure out her next steps. Given that their relationship was over, Morgan didn't want anything from Jared, including his help finding a job. She realized now that wasn't the reason she'd stayed in Austin to begin with. It was because she'd fallen for him.

And now she would have to swallow her pride and ask Dane for help. Morgan would have preferred to be self-sufficient, but beggars couldn't be choosers.

She was finished packing by noon and planned to leave the key with the concierge on her way out. They'd already seen to her luggage so Morgan was giving the apartment one final look and was picking up her carry-on when the doorbell sounded. Morgan didn't need to look through the peephole to know who it was. She just knew.

Jared.

When she'd finally turned on her phone this morning, there had been endless texts and voice mails from Ruth and Morgan's siblings, who'd all read the story and wanted to know if she was okay. And then there were half a dozen voice mails from Jared. She didn't want to talk to him then and didn't intend to now.

But she had to face him one last time. Morgan swung open the door. Jared was leaning against the door frame in faded jeans and a pullover sweater with a bleak look in his eyes.

"Whatever you have to say, I'm not interested."

"We need to talk."

"*We* don't have to do anything." Morgan walked inside her apartment and to her despair, Jared followed. She smelled his spicy scent and it caused a fissure in her chest. But she refused to let her emotions bleed out and make a mess on the floor. "And I was just leaving."

Jared glanced at her small carry-on. "Are you going somewhere?"

"Yes."

"Where?"

"Does it really matter?" Morgan asked. "You have bigger fish to fry, like taking care of your child."

Jared's eyes turned stormy dark. "I don't have a child, Morgan. That's what I came to explain. Ally spewed lies last night. I don't have a child with Samantha. This is all some elaborate media ruse they've concocted, which is why I went to Samantha and told her I want a paternity test."

"Good for you." Morgan grasped her handbag and carry-on and moved to open the door. "I'm sure your family will appreciate that, but I have a flight to catch."

Jared pushed the door closed with the palm of his hand. "You can't leave like this, with so much unfinished between us."

Morgan shook her head. "You've made it pretty clear you're no longer interested in continuing our arrangement or in being my lover. I'm sure it must have been a strain dealing with my lack of knowledge for someone so experienced as yourself, but I got the hint, okay? So please, let me leave gracefully and with a shred of dignity."

She passed underneath his arm, walked to the elevator bank and pressed the down button. Jared followed her.

"You're not even going to give me the benefit of the doubt?" he asked, his expression watchful. "After everything…"

The elevator chimed and Morgan stepped inside. Jared did the same. She couldn't look at him. She didn't dare because Morgan knew if she did, she'd be lost, caught up in his world again where she'd lose herself. Jared was never going to be her Prince Charming. He'd told her from the start and she'd foolishly built him up in her heart to be more.

She'd been wrong.

When the elevator made it to the ground floor, Jared surprised Morgan by taking her carry-on and walking with her through the lobby. But when they reached the French doors he stopped.

"Don't go," he pleaded, halting her steps. "Stay with me. We can figure this out."

"I can't. I can't see you ever again, Jared. It hurts too much." Morgan couldn't take it anymore. She wrenched her bag from his grasp and rushed out the doors. She knew if she didn't leave now she would never leave because Jared had a hold on her.

Morgan wasn't looking where she was going and ran out into the circular driveway just as a car drove up to the entrance. Morgan caught a glimpse of it, but not in time to stop. Her last image as the car struck her was of soaring through the air and Jared's horrified expression before everything went black.

Jared was frozen for several seconds on the sidewalk as he watched Morgan fly through the air and hit the pavement. Then, he sprang into action, rushing to her side. She was unconscious, sprawled out in the driveway, with blood gushing from her head.

He was terrified. He knew enough not to move her with a head injury. "Call an ambulance!" he screamed.

The valet was on his phone immediately while the driver of the car got out and started toward Jared. "Stay away!" He held his hand up.

"I'm so sorry," the man cried. "I didn't see her. She jumped out in front of my car. I tried to…"

"Shut up! I don't give a damn about your excuses." Jared responded. He just prayed Morgan would survive this, but she wasn't moving. He looked down at her and whispered, "Please, baby, please don't leave me."

He lowered his head and rested it against her bosom. It was inconceivable to him that Morgan could leave this earth and he would never see her again. And tell her what he'd only just discovered as she'd hurtled through the air.

"I love you," he said softly against her chest. But feared it was too late.

Twenty

"Jared, what the hell happened?" His grandmother ran toward him in the waiting room of St. David's Medical Center with his parents, Chris and Kandi close behind her. It was the first time in his life he'd ever seen his grandmother disheveled. She was usually so put together, but today, her hair was ruffled and she wore jeans and a tunic. He doubted she'd ever worn jeans a day in her life. "How's Morgan?"

"I—I don't know…" Jared shook his head. "They've been running lots of tests—X-rays, CAT scans and some sort of EEG to record the electrical activity in her brain."

"Omigod!" His grandmother clasped her hand to her mouth, fell into a chair and began sobbing.

"It's okay." His mother rushed to her side. "She's going to pull through."

"Is there anything we can do?" Chris asked and Kandi nodded.

"Morgan's been so great to me," she said, tears in her eyes. "This is so awful." She turned into Chris's arms and wept.

Jared moved away from them to the window and stared blankly outside. He felt a presence behind him and saw his father's reflection in the glass. "I'm sorry, son. I know I was hard on you the other night. And I can see I was wrong. You've changed. You care for this girl."

"It's more than that, Dad," Jared said, turning to face him. "I love her. And I never thought I could feel that way about anybody. But when I saw that car hit her and she went flying through the air—" he shook his head trying to rid himself of the images "—I swear to God, I… I thought…"

His father clutched his shoulders, bringing him into a hug. "Don't say it. Let alone think it." He grasped both sides of Jared's face. "Morgan's a strong woman, okay?"

Jared nodded. "I feel so guilty. She was leaving because of me."

"Perhaps you should feel guilty," a sharp female voice said from behind his father. Jared glanced up and saw Fallon standing there. Her husband Gage, Ayden and his wife, Maya, were by her side. Jared had met them all at Dane's wedding.

On his way in the ambulance, he'd called his parents and then he'd called Dane. When he'd reached him, his friend had been beside himself, but promised to be there as soon as he could. Dane told Jared he'd call the rest of Morgan's siblings.

"Fallon." Chris came toward them. They'd all grown up together, but Chris and Fallon were close in age, like Dane and Jared. "That's not fair. Jared wasn't driving the car that hit Morgan."

"But you hurt her." Fallon's hazel-gray eyes—*Morgan's eyes*—stared back at him accusingly.

"The rumors about Jared fathering a child are a blatant lie," Chris said. Jared appreciated his brother defending him, but Fallon was right. It was because of him Morgan was in this predicament. Maybe if he'd stayed away, she wouldn't be hurt.

Tears sprang to his eyes. "I'm sorry." Jared spun on his heel and walked out of the waiting room and down the hall. He didn't have a particular destination in mind. He just needed breathing room. Everyone in that waiting room knew Morgan was a good woman and wondered why she'd been with a schmuck like him. She'd been leaving because she had cause to believe the rumors were true. He wasn't a good guy.

Or at least he hadn't been.

Until Morgan.

Jared walked aimlessly and found himself at the doors of the small hospital chapel. He didn't know how he got there, but he pushed the doors open and walked inside. It was empty. There were several pews with a cross in the center of the room.

Jared wasn't a religious man, but he sat in one of the pews anyway. If he closed his eyes, he could feel Morgan's lips on his. Picture her smile. She'd imprinted on his heart and he couldn't imagine his life without her.

Clasping his hands together, Jared lowered his head and prayed. He prayed that Morgan would pull through this. There was so much left unsaid between them. He loved her. He'd been afraid to see it. He'd tried to deny and ignore it, but he couldn't deny the truth any longer. She was everything he'd ever wanted and hadn't known he needed. And although he didn't know Morgan's exact feelings, Jared was certain she felt something. If not love, then genuine affection for him. They had a foundation to build on.

He heard the doors of the chapel open, but he didn't look up. He was too caught up in his own guilt. When he turned, it was his brother. Chris sat beside him and wrapped an arm around him. And for the first time in his life, Jared cried. Tears gushed out of his eyes and he let them. If anything happened to Morgan, he'd never forgive himself.

"I've got you, bro," Chris whispered. "I've got you."

Jared didn't know how long they stayed that way, but eventually his tears subsided and he pulled himself together and rose to his feet. He had to get an update on Morgan's condition.

But first he turned to Chris and pointed at him. "If you tell anyone I cried, I'll deny it."

"I would expect nothing less," Chris said. "C'mon." They walked out of the chapel together.

When Jared arrived back at the waiting room he was shocked to see Henry and Nora Stewart there.

"What the hell?"

"Easy, Jared," Chris whispered beside him.

Jared pushed Chris's warning aside. "I'm not going to stay calm. What are you doing here?" He looked at Henry. "You've consistently denied Morgan was your child and rebuffed her attempts to get to know you. If

I recall correctly, you told her you would never accept her as your daughter, would never claim her. So I ask again, why are you here?"

He saw Fallon stand up, but her husband, Gage, gently pushed her back in her chair. Jared didn't care if Fallon was upset. Morgan couldn't speak up for herself, so he would.

Henry lowered his lashes for several moments. "You're right, Jared. I may not have known of her existence before, but once I did, I treated Morgan horribly. I've been a terrible father to her and not just to her, but to my oldest son, Ayden." Henry glanced at Ayden, who was sitting nearby with Maya, glaring at him. "I've never liked admitting I was wrong, that I could make a mistake, but I'm doing it now. I'm truly sorry, and if Morgan pulls through, I'll be a better father."

"That's a little too late," Jared said. "What if…"

"Jared Robinson." His grandmother came up beside him and spun him around. "You will not say such a thing. My girl—" at his raised brow, she amended "—*our* girl will make it. All of us will accept nothing else." She looked sternly at Henry as she said those last words.

Jared nodded and took a seat beside her. Morgan had a lot of people praying for her recovery. Jared hoped it was enough.

Morgan fought to open her eyes, but it was so hard. Her vision was hazy. She couldn't hear, either, except for a low buzzing noise and her entire body throbbed with pain, especially her head. She felt lost and unsure of her surroundings.

Slowly her sight became clear and she saw Dane sitting in a chair beside her with a blanket thrown over him. *What was he doing here? Shouldn't he be in Los Angeles with Iris and Jayden?*

She tried to speak, but realized something was in her mouth and she couldn't talk. Panicking, Morgan tapped the bed to get his attention.

Dane started when he heard the noise. "Morgan?" His brown eyes rested on hers and a large smile spread across his face. "Oh, thank God." He rushed toward her and began kissing her furiously on the forehead. "I'm going to call the nurse to get that tube out of your throat."

There was a tube in her throat? Why?
What happened to her?

Dane ran out of the room and Morgan heard him calling for help. She tried to calm down. Soon nurses and a team of doctors flooded the room. First they removed the breathing tube, then checked her vitals and examined her. They explained she'd been in a coma for a few days. She suffered a brain injury when she'd been hit by a car.

Hit by a car?

Morgan vaguely remembered being in her apartment with Jared and then nothing. Despite her spotty memory, Morgan noticed one thing. Her family had come into the room.

All of them.

It wasn't just Dane. Fallon and Ayden were present with their spouses, but most surprising of all, her father was here with Nora. Morgan stared as the medical team worked around her. *Why was Henry here?* He'd told her he'd never acknowledge her and she'd believed him. It was one of the reasons she'd finally decided to leave Austin. *That much she remembered.*

And then there were the Robinsons. Ruth was beaming at her from the other side of the bed, while Jared's parents, Chris and Kandi enthusiastically smiled at her.

But one person was missing.

The one person she wanted to see more than anyone else, even though she'd told him she was leaving Austin and never wanted to see him again. Even though he may have fathered another woman's baby. Morgan still loved him and wanted to see him.

Jared.

Why were his parents here and not him?

Where was he?

Eventually the doctor turned to the large group assembled. "All right folks, I let you all come in so you could see for yourself Morgan is on the mend, but we're going to need to limit visitors. Morgan's been through quite an ordeal."

"Of course," Ruth said with a small smile. "We'll wait outside." She walked over to Morgan and squeezed her hand. She could see Ruth trying to keep it together, but the old bird had a soft spot because a tear leaked from her eyelid. "We're just so thankful to see you awake."

Morgan nodded because she too was overcome with emotion to speak. She watched as the Robinsons filed out of the room. Now only the Stewarts remained.

Her father came toward her bed. "I'd like to speak to Morgan alone if I may?" He glanced back at his children and their spouses. Ayden, Dane and Fallon looked back and forth at each other, clearly uneasy with their father's request.

Fallon spoke up. "I don't know, Dad. Perhaps this reunion can wait?"

Henry shook his head. "I'm sorry. It can't wait another minute."

Fallon looked at Morgan, asking an unspoken question.

"It's okay," Morgan croaked. "I'll hear him out."

"We'll be right outside the door if you need us," Dane said. Several moments later, her siblings and their spouses all exited the room, leaving Morgan alone with Henry and Nora.

Surprisingly, Henry turned to his wife, who stood woodenly at his side. Nora looked no worse for wear in jeans and a white button-down shirt, though Morgan did notice she wasn't as made up as she'd seen Nora in the past.

"That includes you too, darling," Henry stated softly. "I need to talk to my daughter alone."

"Henry…"

He gave Nora a look that said the topic wasn't up for discussion. Begrudgingly, Nora left the room. Henry pulled up the chair Dane had vacated to Morgan's beside.

Morgan didn't know how to feel having Henry here. After all the years of wanting and dreaming of a father, when she'd finally revealed herself, he'd cast her aside. He'd made her feel less than, as if she wasn't good enough to have his blood running through her veins.

"Morgan, I'm sorry."

"Exactly what are you sorry for?" A couple of instances came to mind such as his cold words when she'd confronted him at Stewart Manor and he'd told her, "I owe you nothing." Or perhaps it was the angry glare he'd given her at the Alzheimer's charity event. She may have forgotten some things, but not his hostility toward her.

"For everything. I've treated you abominably."

Morgan's hearted contracted and the machines hooked up to her began to beat erratically as her blood pressure spiked. "Yeah, you did."

Henry touched her hand and Morgan flinched, so he pulled away. "Please calm down. I don't want you upset."

"Your being here is upsetting."

His features contracted and Morgan knew she'd hurt him. "I was hoping for the opposite effect. I know I was wrong. I pushed you away when I should have been pulling you closer."

Tears sprang to her eyes and she only had one thing to say. "Why?"

Henry rubbed his hands together and she could see he was mulling over his words. He was silent for several beats and then he spoke. "Because I thought I was a better man with Nora. Or at least I was going to try to be after my marriage to Lillian ended badly. But one night in Vegas I messed up. Nora and I had been going through a rough patch in our marriage and I was feeling lonely. Neglected. There's no excuse, but I met a beautiful showgirl and we became intimate. I regretted it soon after it happened and I went back to Nora more determined than ever to make our marriage work. And I did. We got through it."

Morgan stared back at Henry. She was finally getting an explanation for his behavior, but she suspected it wasn't going to bring her the comfort she thought it would.

"I'd put that evening with your mother behind me and never thought of it again," Henry said. "It was as if it never happened. But then you showed up at Dane's wedding and told me you were a result of that night when I was at my lowest. I wasn't just angry. I was embarrassed at being faced with my greatest failure as a man, *as a husband.*"

So Nora was right, Morgan thought. He thought of Morgan as a mistake. "Please stop. I don't want to hear any more." He was nailing the coffin shut on their ever having a relationship.

"Morgan, please. Let me say this. You deserve an explanation."

Morgan shook her head. "It hurts too much."

"And I'm sorry for that," Henry said. "I lashed out at you when the person I was angry at most with was myself because you were the next best target. It wasn't your fault I cheated on Nora. *I* did that. You were an innocent child who deserved to have a father, but I swear to you, I had no idea you'd been conceived. Your mother never reached out to me after that night, but then again we hadn't exchanged much info. Had I known…"

"You would have acknowledged me?" Morgan snorted with derision. "Like you did Ayden? You were married to his mother, for Christ's sake. Please don't lie."

Henry rose to his feet and began to pace, then stopped and turned back to her. "You're right. I've been a selfish bastard trying to hold on to my wealth and my young wife. I've treated you and Ayden horribly and I can't take those moments back, Morgan. All I can tell you is that I want to try to make it right. I want to heal the divide between me and my children. I intend to embrace all of my heirs, including you. If you still want that."

Morgan was speechless. She'd waited a lifetime to hear a father say he wanted to be part of her life, but she was scared to reach for the brass ring. *What if he pulled the rug out from under her because she didn't measure up?* Morgan wasn't sure she could trust him with her heart.

"I don't know if I can believe you," Morgan responded. "You talk a good game, but actions speak louder than words."

"I know I don't deserve it and you have every right to tell me to take a hike after the way I've treated you, but I'm asking if you will give me a chance to be a father." Henry's eyes were watering. "I will work on making it up to you. I promise. I just need to know if you'll give me another shot."

Tears slid down Morgan's cheek. Out of spite, she wanted to tell him no. To be as mean and hateful as he'd been to her. But deep down all she'd ever wanted was to have a dad. To have someone save her from the awful life she'd endured with her mother and all those men. To have a father to kiss away the boo-boos and make it all better.

Being angry with Henry wouldn't hurt just him. It would hurt her too. If she didn't forgive him, she'd never really heal and be able to move on with her life. Or have a good relationship with a man because didn't a women's first relationship start with her father?

Morgan nodded. "All right."

Henry's hazel-gray eyes became cloudy as he reached for Morgan and she reluctantly allowed him to hold her in his embrace. "Oh, thank God. I'm not too late." He leaned back and kissed the top of her head. "I'm sorry, baby girl. I'm so sorry, but Daddy's got you."

Henry held Morgan in his arms and it was wonderful knowing she was finally accepted. She belonged.

Twenty-One

Jared ran through the corridors of St. David's Medical Center after Chris texted him Morgan was awake. Of course it happened when he'd left the hospital for an hour. He'd gotten a call from the lab that the results of the paternity test were in. While he'd waited for Morgan to wake up, he and Samantha's daughter had had blood drawn. Jared had to know the truth, so he'd gone personally to get the results. When Morgan awoke— and he'd believed she would—he wanted to have the paternity results to show her the truth. To show her he wasn't like Henry and would never abandon his child.

And he was right.

The results said with one hundred percent certainty that he couldn't have fathered Samantha's child. He'd already called Ally's boss and threatened him with a lawsuit over slandering Jared's name. The blog had a retraction being prepared, which would go live that afternoon. In time, the brouhaha would die down, but Jared was furious because he could have lost Morgan because of it.

Jared was relieved as he'd driven back to the hospital. Then Chris had given him the good news Morgan was awake, but he wasn't there. Jared felt terrible. He'd wanted to be the first person Morgan saw when she awoke. Hopefully, seeing the Stewarts there would help salve the wound. Because if he was honest, would she really want to see him?

Would she remember she'd told him they were over and she never wanted to see him again?

He hoped not, but even if she did, Jared planned on convincing Morgan he would never leave her side. He couldn't wait to tell her just how much he loved her.

On his way to Morgan's room, he stopped by the waiting room. His family and the Stewarts were all assembled.

"Jared! Thank heavens you're here." His grandmother smiled when she saw him. "Morgan is awake."

Jared grinned. "I know, and I'm headed to see her, but I wanted to share some news." He held up the envelope in his hands. "Results of the paternity test showing I *didn't* father a child."

He noticed Fallon raise her hands up to the sky in silent thanks.

"I never doubted you," Chris said, coming to Jared and giving him a hug.

"We may have." Ayden glanced at Fallon and Dane. "I'm glad that we were wrong." He came forward and offered his hand. Jared shook it. He knew Morgan's siblings only wanted the best for her. But he was that man and it was time their sister knew it.

"Thank you," Jared said. "Now, if you'll excuse me. I need to see someone."

"Go get her, tiger!" Kandi yelled from the sidelines as Jared quickly walked down the corridor to Morgan's room. When he arrived, the door was partially open and to his surprise, Henry had Morgan wrapped in his arms. He didn't want to interrupt the reunion, but Henry caught sight of him and motioned him forward.

"Come in, Jared. I think someone might like to see you." He pulled away and Jared's eyes connected with Morgan's. His heart expanded at finally seeing her awake after so many days of praying for her recovery.

Henry glanced at Jared and back at Morgan. "I'm going to give you both some privacy."

Jared was speechless and merely nodded. Henry patted him on the shoulder as he left and whispered, "Don't give up on her."

Jared stood by the doorway after he left, afraid to step forward.

"Are you just going to stand there?" Morgan asked.

At her words, Jared sprang into action, walking toward the bed and sitting in the chair beside her. "Morgan, I… I'm so thankful you're okay," he barely managed to get out.

She nodded.

"How much do you remember? Of the accident?"

"Not much," Morgan answered. "The doctors said, my memory could come back today, in pieces or not at all. And I don't much care if it does. I don't want to remember being hit by a car." She gave a half laugh. "But I do recall telling you I was leaving Austin for good."

Her words hit Jared's ears like the crash that had almost taken her from him and his heart sank. "I was hoping you'd forget that part."

Morgan sighed. "Not likely." She stared at him. "I know we need to talk, but I have to say this first. Thank you."

"For what?"

"For calling my family," Morgan replied. "It's because of you they're all here. Henry—I mean, my father—told me you called Dane and he rallied everyone. And as you can see—" she motioned to the door and he could see tears glistening in her eyelids "—I'm going to have the family I always wanted. So thank you."

Jared swallowed the lump in his throat, but it remained lodged in his chest. "You already have a family, Morgan. Me and all the Robinsons. Please tell me you know that."

Morgan stared into Jared's beautiful dark eyes, eyes she'd come to know so well. It appeared as if he hadn't gotten much sleep. Instead of his usual tidy appearance, Jared looked haggard with several days' stubble on his chiseled jaw. He was wearing a simple T-shirt and dark stonewashed jeans. But in her opinion, he'd never looked sexier. Handsome didn't come close to describing his lethal good looks.

She'd been disappointed when she hadn't seen him among all her visitors, but he was here now and she wanted to weep with gratitude. "When I woke up and you weren't here…"

"Sweetheart." Jared jumped out of the chair and onto the edge of Morgan's bed. "I've been by your side day and night driving the doctors and nurses crazy. The only reason I left was for this." He pulled out the manila envelope from his back pocket.

Morgan frowned. "What's that?"

"The results of the paternity test," Jared replied. "Showing I'm not a father."

Morgan lowered her lashes. "I know."

His eyes widened in surprise and a faint smile touched his mouth. "You do? But you said…"

"I was hurt and in my feelings." She glanced up and felt her eyes swim with tears while her mouth trembled "I—I thought you didn't want me and I latched on to the first thing I heard that validated that premise. But I know you, Jared." Morgan reached out and pressed her hand to his cheek, smiling when he closed his eyes and let her caress him. "I know you're not the kind of man who would abandon his child. I *know* that."

She heard his audible sigh of relief. "Thank you. So if you can believe that much about me, can you believe one more thing?"

She shrugged. "Maybe?"

"I love you, Morgan."

Joy careened through her, but Morgan had to be sure she wasn't hearing things. "What did you say?"

"I love you." Jared gazed into her eyes for a long, lingering moment.

Astonished and struck speechless by his confession, Morgan looked back at him.

"I'm *in love* with you. You're the first thing I think about in the morning and the last thing I think about at night. And it scared me to feel that much, never mind admitting to it. So I kept my distance because I was afraid I couldn't be the Prince Charming you'd built me up to be. I thought I wasn't good enough for someone as beautiful, sweet and kind as you."

"Oh Jared…"

"I've never been in love, Morgan. I made a mess of things last week with you, but I know what I feel now. Seeing you nearly die in front of me, everything in my world went gray and I knew I couldn't live a day without you. I realized how precious life was and that I didn't want to waste another minute. I promised myself if you pulled through that I would confess my love. Because when I'm with you, Morgan, my whole world is brighter, lighter and filled with love."

Morgan had dreamed of this moment, but never thought it was possible Jared could feel the same way about her as she felt about him. "I feel the same way, Jared."

"You do?" His mouth curved into a smile.

Morgan smiled through her tears. "I love you too." And she loved the way his gleaming dark eyes pulsed as she said the words. "I think I have from the moment we met. If you had told me you could fall in love at first sight, I would have told you, you watched too many Dane Stewart romantic comedies, but it's true. I love you."

Jared framed her face with his hands, bringing her closer to him so her forehead rested on his. They stayed that way for several moments, neither of them speaking, just soaking in the emotion of what they'd revealed to one another. A deep happiness Morgan hadn't known was possible spread through her.

Jared lifted his head and stared deeply into her eyes, allowing her to see the depth of his soul. "Is spending the rest of your life with me something you would consider?"

Morgan tried to hold it together, but her emotions were all over the place after her reunion with her father.

"I want to be with you now and always, Morgan, and that's not ever going to change. So let me try this again." Jared slid out of her grasp and onto one knee by her hospital bed. "Morgan Stewart, would you do me the honor of becoming my wife?"

"Yes, yes, yes," Morgan bent down to lift him up and the machines beside her bed went haywire. She didn't care—she cupped Jared's face and kissed him with breathless, urgent kisses. When they finally parted, she murmured. "You're my beginning and my ending, Jared. You're my everything."

Epilogue

Three months later

"To Jared and Morgan!" Henry raised a glass to toast Morgan and Jared after their wedding at Stewart Manor.

"To Jared and Morgan." Everyone's voices rang out in the backyard near the terrace. Jared clinked his glass against Morgan's and she beamed up at him.

He hoped the day had been everything Morgan dreamed of. It was a small intimate gathering: the Stewarts, the Robinsons and a few close friends. Morgan had looked spectacular in her designer gown. The crystal bodice sheath with the silk tulle skirt had fit her figure like a glove and Jared couldn't wait to take it off later.

Fallon was Morgan's maid of honor while her friend

Whitney and Dane's wife, Iris, served as her brides-
maids. Morgan had wanted Kandi too, but at eight
months, his sister-in-law was very pregnant with his
brother's child and not inclined to stand on her feet all
day. Jared had been proud to have Dane and Ayden
as his groomsmen standing alongside Chris, his best
man. He couldn't have asked for a better entourage. As
married men, Chris and Dane had both offered him
some sage advice.

Happy wife, happy life.

Jared planned on ensuring that, which was why he
had a special surprise in store for Morgan for their
wedding night.

He ambled close to her. "Have I told you lately how
incredibly happy you've made me?"

"Not lately," she said, flirting. "How about you
start."

He lowered his head and pressed his lips to hers and
knew he'd finally come home.

Morgan enjoyed Jared's kiss, but they were interrupted by her nephew Dylan tugging on Jared's tuxedo.

Morgan watched Jared lift him in his arms. He was
going to make a great father someday.

Thinking of fathers had Morgan reflecting on the
highlight of her day: Henry walking her down the aisle.
They had come a long way in their relationship since
her accident. Henry hadn't lied when he told her he'd
be there and wanted to heal the rift with all his children. It had been a toss-up between him and Jared as
to whom she was going to stay with after her recovery. In the end, she decided to be with her man, but

she visited Henry often and they were slowly getting to know each other.

"What are you thinking about?" Jared asked from her side after Dylan went off to play with his cousin Jayden.

Morgan glanced up at Jared and saw love shining in his eyes. "I was thinking about how perfect our wedding was."

"It was perfect, because you finally became mine, all mine. And I can't wait to get you alone," he growled.

Jared's appetite for Morgan hadn't waned. In fact, it was stronger than it had ever been and she was ready for their honeymoon to begin. "What do you say we get out of here?" she murmured.

"Gladly."

They were nearly to the terrace doors when Ruth came forward to kiss Morgan on each cheek. "I'm so happy to officially have you as part of our family. I knew from day one Jared had a keeper."

"So did I," Jared said with a wide grin. "Now, if you'll excuse us…"

"Are you two sneaking off?" she whispered.

Jared nodded.

"All right then, I've got you covered." She winked at them conspiratorially.

Morgan and Jared slipped away without anyone else noticing their departure. They slid into a Bentley minutes later and let it take them the thirty-minute ride to the Robinson family compound. They'd decided to honeymoon there because it was the place they'd fallen for each other.

Jared carried Morgan over the threshold of the cottage where they'd first made love and placed her on her feet. Dozens of candles adorned every surface of the room and rose petals were strewn across the floor leading a path to the bedroom.

Morgan looked at Jared. "You had all this done?"

Jared shrugged. "With a little help from Antoine."

"You're an incredible man, Jared Robinson, and I adore you."

"The feeling's mutual," he murmured. "Now come here, woman." He took her by the hand and led her to the bedroom where they stripped each other naked and came together in a meeting of mind, body and souls. Ecstasy soon swallowed them and they shuddered in simultaneous orgasm. Morgan suspected their rapture had created a miracle.

It proved true several weeks later when a home test showed positive and her doctor confirmed Morgan was pregnant with Jared's baby.

"Are you happy?" Morgan asked when Jared drew her into his embrace after she'd finished dressing at the doctor's office. She was shaking.

"Deliriously," Jared said, smiling down at her. "I can't wait to have a little Morgan running around. She will be Daddy's little girl."

Morgan grinned from ear to ear. "I love you, Jared."

And she did. Loving him had enriched her and now they would have a new life to share theirs with.

It didn't get any better than this.

* * * * *

*Don't miss a single story
in The Stewart Heirs series
by Yahrah St. John!*

At the CEO's Pleasure
His Marriage Demand
Red Carpet Redemption
Secrets of a Fake Fiancée

*Available exclusively
from Harlequin Desire.*

WE HOPE YOU ENJOYED
THIS BOOK FROM

(H) HARLEQUIN
DESIRE

*Luxury, scandal, desire—welcome to
the lives of the American elite.*

Be transported to the worlds of oil barons, family dynasties,
moguls and celebrities. Get ready for juicy plot twists,
delicious sensuality and intriguing scandal.

6 NEW BOOKS AVAILABLE EVERY MONTH!

COMING NEXT MONTH FROM

HARLEQUIN
DESIRE

Available June 2, 2020

#2737 THE PRICE OF PASSION
Texas Cattleman's Club: Rags to Riches • by Maureen Child
Rancher Camden Guthrie is back in Royal, Texas, looking to rebuild his life as a member of the Texas Cattleman's Club. The one person who can help him? Beth Wingate, his ex. Their reunion is red-hot, but startling revelations threaten their future.

#2738 FORBIDDEN LUST
Dynasties: Seven Sins • by Karen Booth
Allison Randall has long desired playboy Zane Patterson. The problem? He's her brother's best friend, and Zane won't betray that bond, no matter how much he wants her. Stranded in paradise, sparks fly, but Allison has a secret that could tear them apart...

#2739 UPSTAIRS DOWNSTAIRS TEMPTATION
The Men of Stone River • by Janice Maynard
Working in an isolated mansion, wealthy widower Farrell Stone needs a live-in housekeeper. Ivy Danby is desperate for a job to support her baby. Their simmering attraction for one another is evident, but are their differences too steep a hurdle to create a future together?

#2740 HOT NASHVILLE NIGHTS
Daughters of Country • by Sheri WhiteFeather
Brooding songwriter Spencer Riggs is ready to reinvent himself. His ex, Alice McKenzie, is the perfect stylist for the job. Years after their wild and passionate romance, Alice finally has her life on track, but will their sizzling attraction burn them both again?

#2741 SCANDALOUS ENGAGEMENT
Lockwood Lightning • by Jules Bennett
To protect her from a relentless ex, restauranteur Reese Conrad proposes to his best friend, Josie Coleman. But their fake engagement reveals real feelings, and Josie sees Reese in a whole new way. And just as things heat up, a shocking revelation changes everything!

#2742 BACK IN HIS EX'S BED
Murphy International • by Joss Wood
Art historian Finn Murphy has a wild, impulsive side. It's what his ex-wife, Beah Jenkinson, found so attractive—and what burned down their white-hot marriage. Now, reunited to plan a friend's wedding, the chemistry is still there... and so are the problems that broke them apart.

SPECIAL EXCERPT FROM

⊕ HARLEQUIN

DESIRE

*To protect her from a relentless ex, restaurateur Reese
Conrad proposes to his best friend, Josie Coleman.
But their fake engagement reveals real feelings, and
Josie sees Reese in a whole new way. And just as things
heat up, a shocking revelation changes everything!*

Read on for a sneak peek at
Scandalous Engagement
by USA TODAY *bestselling author Jules Bennett.*

"What's that smile for?" he asked.

She circled the island and placed a hand over his heart. "You're
just remarkable. I mean, I've always known, but lately you're just
proving yourself more and more."

He released the wine bottle and covered her hand with his…and
that's when she remembered the kiss. She shouldn't have touched
him—she should've kept her distance because there was that look
in his eyes again. Where had this come from? When did he start
looking at her like he wanted to rip her clothes off and have his
naughty way with her?

"We need to talk about it," he murmured.

It. As if saying the word *kiss* would somehow make this situation
weirder. And as if she hadn't thought of anything else since *it* had
happened.

"Nothing to talk about," she told him, trying to ignore the warmth
and strength between his hand and his chest.

"You can't say you weren't affected."

"I didn't say that."

He tipped his head, somehow making that penetrating stare even
more potent. "It felt like more than a friend kiss."

Way to state the obvious.

"And more than just a practice," he added.

Josie's heart kicked up. They were too close, talking about things that were too intimate. No matter what she felt, what she thought she wanted, this wasn't right. She couldn't ache for her best friend in such a physical way. If that kiss changed things, she couldn't imagine how anything more would affect this relationship.

"We can't go there again," she told him. "I mean, you're a good kisser—"

"Good? That kiss was a hell of a lot better than just good."

She smiled. "Fine. It was pretty incredible. Still, we can't get caught up in this whole fake-engagement thing and lose sight of who we really are."

His free hand came up and brushed her hair away from her face. "I haven't lost sight of anything. And I'm well aware of who we are…and what I want."

Why did that sound so menacing in the most delicious of ways? Why was her body tingling so much from such simple touches when she'd firmly told herself to not get carried away?

Wait. Was he leaning in closer?

"Reese, what are you doing?" she whispered.

"Testing a theory."

His mouth grazed hers like a feather. Her knees literally weakened as she leaned against him for support. Reese continued to hold her hand against his chest, but he wrapped the other arm around her waist, urging her closer.

There was no denying the sizzle or spark or whatever the hell was vibrating between them. She'd always thought those cheesy expressions were so silly, but there was no perfect way to describe such an experience.

And kissing her best friend was quite an experience…

Don't miss what happens next in…
Scandalous Engagement
by USA TODAY bestselling author Jules Bennett.

Available June 2020 wherever
Harlequin Desire books and ebooks are sold.

Harlequin.com

Get 4 FREE REWARDS!

We'll send you 2 FREE Books plus <u>2 FREE Mystery Gifts.</u>

Harlequin Desire® books transport you to the world of the American elite with juicy plot twists, delicious sensuality and intriguing scandal.

FREE
Value Over
$20

YES! Please send me 2 FREE Harlequin Desire novels and my 2 FREE gifts (gifts are worth about $10 retail). After receiving them, if I don't wish to receive any more books, I can return the shipping statement marked "cancel." If I don't cancel, I will receive 6 brand-new novels every month and be billed just $4.55 per book in the U.S. or $5.24 per book in Canada. That's a savings of at least 13% off the cover price! It's quite a bargain! Shipping and handling is just 50¢ per book in the U.S. and $1.25 per book in Canada.* I understand that accepting the 2 free books and gifts places me under no obligation to buy anything. I can always return a shipment and cancel at any time. The free books and gifts are mine to keep no matter what I decide.

225/326 HDN GNND

Name (please print)

Address   Apt. #

City   State/Province   Zip/Postal Code

Mail to the **Reader Service:**
IN U.S.A.: P.O. Box 1341, Buffalo, NY 14240-8531
IN CANADA: P.O. Box 603, Fort Erie, Ontario L2A 5X3

Want to try 2 free books from another series! Call 1-800-873-8635 or visit www.ReaderService.com.

---

*Terms and prices subject to change without notice. Prices do not include sales taxes, which will be charged (if applicable) based on your state or country of residence. Canadian residents will be charged applicable taxes. Offer not valid in Quebec. This offer is limited to one order per household. Books received may not be as shown. Not valid for current subscribers to Harlequin Desire books. All orders subject to approval. Credit or debit balances in a customer's account(s) may be offset by any other outstanding balance owed by or to the customer. Please allow 4 to 6 weeks for delivery. Offer available while quantities last.

Your Privacy—The Reader Service is committed to protecting your privacy. Our Privacy Policy is available online at www.ReaderService.com or upon request from the Reader Service. We make a portion of our mailing list available to reputable third parties that offer products we believe may interest you. If you prefer that we not exchange your name with third parties, or if you wish to clarify or modify your communication preferences, please visit us at www.ReaderService.com/consumerschoice or write to us at Reader Service Preference Service, P.O. Box 9062, Buffalo, NY 14240-9062. Include your complete name and address.

HD20R

4949